Edward Henry Bickersteth

The Two Brothers

And Other Poems

Edward Henry Bickersteth

The Two Brothers
And Other Poems

ISBN/EAN: 9783744649827

Printed in Europe, USA, Canada, Australia, Japan

Cover: Foto ©Andreas Hilbeck / pixelio.de

More available books at **www.hansebooks.com**

THE TWO BROTHERS,

And other Poems,

By EDWARD HENRY BICKERSTETH, M.A.

AUTHOR OF "YESTERDAY, TO-DAY, AND FOR EVER."

RIVINGTONS,

London, Oxford, and Cambridge.

1871.

PREFACE.

THE following Poems have been written from time to time during the last twenty-seven years, and have many of them appeared in print before; but being for the most part now inaccessible to friends who kindly continue to ask for them, I have ventured to group them in this volume. Some of them are here published for the first time. The dates, which are affixed to most of the Poems, will enable the reader to assign the lighter pieces to my early home and college days. May He who directs the wind-borne seed to the genial soil only plant a few winged words in some hearts, where they shall not be wholly unfruitful, and my hopes will be abundantly fulfilled.

E. H. B.

CHRIST CHURCH VICARAGE,
Hampstead, 1871.

CONTENTS.

THE TWO BROTHERS.

Εὔδουσα γὰρ φρὴν ὄμμασιν λαμπρύνεται.

ÆSCH. *Eum.*

ARE the embers smouldering, brother? Think not to revive
    their light.
Brother, I've a tale to tell thee I can better tell at night:
And their faint dun glow will glimmer till, perchance, my
    tale is done.
List!—that dull and heavy sound—it is the church-bell
    pealing 'one.'
Strangely through the sere elm forests come the fitful gusts
    of wind,
Strangely on the casement beats the hollow drifting rain
    behind;
Night broods round, a wall of darkness, such as moonbeams
    cannot scale,
And the blessed stars are blunted like a shaft from coat of
    mail.

B

Thirteen summers have waved round us, thirteen winters
    shower'd their snows,

Thirteen springs danced by, and thirteen autumns pass'd
    like music's close,

Since I witness'd gloom like this, wherein the stoutest heart
    would melt:

Thick close darkness on our eyelids weighing—darkness
    that is felt.

Oh, the memory of that midnight, spectre-like, within me
    sleeps;

If I only gaze, it rises dimly from my spirit's deeps—

Rises with the sere elm forests struck by fitful gusts of
    wind,

And the hollow drifting raindrops on the casement close
    behind:

Every wind-moan finds an echo in my moaning heart within,

And the rain is not as dewdrops to a soul once scarr'd with
    sin.

Brother, thou wert ever to me as a young and golden mist

Floating through blue liquid heavens, with the morning sun-
    light kiss'd;

Which the eye looks up and blesses, lingering on its track
above,

With an old familiar fondness and an earnestness of love.

Brother, I to thee was ever as a storm-cloud on the hills,

Lowering o'er the rocks and caverns and the laughter of the
rills:

Yet I've thought at times, my brother, from the sunshine of
thy life,

Passing rainbow gleams have fallen on my spirit-world of
strife:

For when every fount was wormwood, every star had ceased
to shine,

It was bliss in dreams to ponder how unlike thy lot to
mine.

Yet, in childhood, I remember how our sainted mother
said—

Often on bright Sabbath eves, and thrice upon her dying
bed—

That far scenes would crowd upon her, when she look'd on
me and thee,

In the distance, dream-like dawning, from the glorious
dream-countree.

She was kneeling, as she told us, at her Saviour's blessed feet—

Leaning on her harp, which warbled (as she knelt) heaven's
    music sweet—

But the thrill of that communion, and the smiles that on
    her fell,

And the melody of worship, words, she said, might never tell

Still the dream grew clear and clearer, softer still that music's
    tone,

And she saw she was not kneeling in that glorious light alone

For beside her were two spirits (well she knew them), I and
    thou ;

Life and light and love, all blended, like soft rainbows, on
    our brow.

And like us in blest communion kneeling, singing as we sung

On the hand of each of us a gentler lovelier angel hung.

Often since I've mused, my brother, when my heart was
    rent, if this

Were a heaven-sent dream, prophetic of a far-off home of bliss

Or a beautiful life-picture by affection's fingers drawn,

But which, like my earthly joys, should fade, fade, fade away
    at dawn.

Weep not, brother! thou hast found that angel of the far-off
    land,

Whom our mother saw there kneeling, gently clinging to
    thy hand.

I, too, have a tale to tell thee (would that it may end in
    light),

Though a tale of sin and sorrow, I can better tell at night.

Who could speak of sad hearts broken by himself, of tear-
    drown'd eyes,

And of wither'd hopes and feelings, underneath blue laughing
    skies ?

Sorrow clings to sorrow's raiment—grief must have her
    twilight wan—

Moan, ye winds and woods and waves, and let the embers
    smoulder on.

Gaze with me a moment down the billowy ocean of our life,

Which with tears and fitful radiance seems mysteriously rife:

In the distance, like the earliest flush of morning o'er the
    hills,

Even here, through cloud and gloom, a dewy mellow light
    distils.

Still it grows upon my sight intensely beautiful and grand,

From the land of childhood streaming, childhood's golden
    faery-land :

When Time went on sunshine wheels, on wings of breezy
    joyaunce by,

Every feeling, like the sky-lark, from the earth and to the
    sky.

Then, perchance, no human seer that look'd upon our reck-
    less brow,

Could have prophesied the diverse pathway we are travelling
    now.

But the first black cloud that shadow'd childhood's blue
    pellucid years,

Gloom'd, rose, cover'd, broke upon us with a sudden dash of
    tears—

Gloom'd upon the morn, the tidings of our father's victory
    came,

Earn'd with precious drops of blood—the dew, an' if ye will,
    of fame;

Broke—the next sad post a letter, edged with black, too
    surely told

That his heart was still for ever, and his lips for ever cold.

Then our mother—day by day she struggled with her choking
    grief—

Oh, she could not—but beside us wither'd, like a dying leaf :

And, when leaves should die, in autumn, her the first of all
    the year,

Laid we down, with sighs and weeping, on her cold sepul-
    chral bier;

And with faltering listless footsteps slowly sought, when all
    was o'er,

Hand in hand our desolate home; though desolate, ours, alas,
    no more.

We were parted—each alone, 'mid stranger hearts and faces
    strange:

Dreary seem'd the waste of lifetime, like a barren shore, to
    range.

But a gentle eye fell on thee—seem'd it but a sister's love ?

Pity's tears, that wept thy sorrows, from one tenderer than
    the dove ?

Oh, ye grew for five brief summers there together, side by
    side,

Till she stood in beauty by thee, thine own loving lovely
    bride;

Blushing, trembling, till the vow to love thee—then her face
    grew bright,
And intense affection o'er her threw a beauty like the light.
Ah! how beautiful life's ocean seem'd that gentle cloudless
    noon,
Like a moonlight sea that slumbers underneath the summer
    moon,
When the stars steal hearts responsive to their own wild
    eloquence,
And a strange sweet music o'er us comes, we know not, heed
    not, whence,—
From the skies, or from the falling of melodious drops of
    foam,
Or from deeper spirit-fountains welling in our spirit-home.
Few, methinks, are such blest havens on the shores of time
    and earth ;
Seldom broods there peace so tranquil over life's exuberant
    mirth.

But I must not linger, brother, on the brightness of thy track,
When dark spectres round mine own with spells are whisper-
    ing me back.

List ! I do not wish that others should partake my sinful load,

Yet I sometimes think the streamlet from that bitter fountain flow'd:

For when harsh unkindness pruned and stunted all affection's shoots,

Then perhaps the canker enter'd, festering at my being's roots:

For with sickening heart I turn'd from human faces, as from blight,

Since they never lit with love, and never read my feelings right,

To the world of thought and fancy—that, my country—books, my friends ;

Fool, fool ! deeming heartless things for gushing hearts would make amends.

Yet at first how strangely lovely seem'd that icy crystal air,

To a lonely nestless bird upon its first wild entrance there.

Day by day the spirit finding eagle strength within its wings,

Proudly tracking truth and beauty there 'mid everlasting things ;

Never pausing, resting never on its flight intensely keen,

Deeming it would touch the boundary of that dark-blue vault serene.

If I gazed below, the mists were wrapping all in vaporous
 fold,

Mists of selfishness and meanness, chilling blight, and sordid
 gold:

All along whose cloudy skirts base ignis-fatuus lights would
 flame,

Luxury, and ease, and riches, and perhaps some petty
 fame.

"Let them flame and flare," I shouted, "round those spirits'
 prison bars,

"Mine are the free boundless heavens, mine the lightnings,
 mine the stars :"

And aloft I clapp'd my pinions, soaring on for days and
 weeks,

After some fresh burning hope still kindling o'er fresh
 mountain-peaks.

Ah, I knew not that, though earthborn lamps might never
 mount so high,

There are meteors that deceive, and stars[1] that wander in
 the sky.

[1] ἀστέρες πλανῆται.—Jude 13.

Ah, I saw not that the pole-star, Faith, was waning fast and
    dim,

And of God—fool, fool!—I thought not in my madden'd
    heart of Him ;

But from far I heard a whisper of the fontal light divine,

Reason, human earthly Reason, sheds within the spirit's
    shrine.

Syren-like that music falling, like a gush of holy tears

On deep waves, flow'd on and whisper'd 'twas the music of
    the spheres,

Bidding me come up and follow to its own dear home on high,

Maddening while it tranced my soul, and blinding while it
    lured mine eye ;

Till I rear'd my adoration higher than God's eternal throne ;—

Reason was the God I worshipp'd—trusting, clinging there
    alone.

And I follow'd—poor fond climber—leaving faith and trust
    above

To low grovelling minds of earth, or fond enthusiasts' frantic
    love,

Till I stood in naked horror on the sceptic's precipice,

All my darling visions staring on me there, like things of ice.

Oh, the solitude that crush'd me! oh, that dreary word
    'alone'!

Not a kindred heart to lean on, not an anchor for mine own—

Without truth and love and beauty, human love or love of
    God—

Not a gleam to point the pathway of return the way I
    trode :—

But the meteors, I had follow'd, sicken'd one by one and died,

And the dark[2] of darkness o'er them closed for ever far and
    wide,

Woe was me! for in that midnight I could neither pray nor
    weep—

Had I pray'd an Ear was open, and an Eye that could not
    sleep.

But when all without was desert, and wild desert all within,

Plunged I with a maniac's madness, down the treacherous
    gulph of sin.

Whilome I had often sneer'd at others from the height of
    fame,

Finding what they deem'd enjoyment in the haunts of sin and
    shame ;—

---

[2] οἷς ὁ ζόφος τοῦ σκότους εἰς αἰῶνα τετήρηται.—Jude 13.

Now—but no—I will not drag thee to the gloomy dens of
    guilt—

List! their spectral voices haunt me—go and ask them if
    thou wilt:

Broken hearts and gentle bosoms, once serene and pure as
    thine—

Woe, woe! broken now and withering soon to fall and die
    like mine—

But I reck'd not, for my spirit seem'd alternate fire and
    night,

Like a cloud-robed sky at midnight riven and kindled into
    light.

Hush! speak low: how shall I tell thee after this of inno-
    cence?

Thou wilt mock me—brother, brother—I can never tell
    thee—hence!

See! the embers all have smoulder'd—see their faint light
    dying wanes:

Brother, look, a star is trembling through the tearful win-
    dow-panes.

I can tell thee now,—for blessed are to me the thoughts
      that rise

With those silent pilgrims yonder wending through the
      silent skies.

Even thus amid the darkness, and the winds, the waves, the
      storm,

Of my sin-sick soul, I pass'd one evening by an angel form.

She had seen me sadly smile upon some children sporting by,

And her heart was touch'd with pity—and a tear came in her
      eye :

And she look'd upon me—spell-bound, I stood still and
      look'd on her,

And a gleam of light fell glancing down the mists of things
      that were.

Surely ne'er o'er human bosom came love in such tempest-kind;

All my spirit's dark foundations heaved like waves beneath
      the wind.

Often did I wrench the thought from out my bosom's core
      and cry,

Never should my cloud-tost being cross that blue trans-
      parent sky.

But again she pass'd, and sighing—*Jesus,* it was all she said.

Yet down, down into her heart-depths through bewildering
    tears I read—

" Thou art weary, way-worn, storm-tost—darker spots are
    on thy soul:

" Jesus died—fear not, dear wanderer—storms must bend to
    His control."

Oh, that word! I scarce had heard it since in music erst it fell

From our sainted mother's lips, who breathed it as her last
    farewell.

The dark thunder-clouds that long had risen with every
    rising day,

Heard it, and were troubled—heard it, and began to break
    away.

Bitter was the shame, and bitter were the first tears that I
    wept;—

Frequent still wild night-mare visions broke upon the sleep
    I slept:—

But at length the spring was heal'd, and gentle tears began
    to flow,

And One whisper'd, "I have suffer'd—I have borne thy
    load of woe !"

All the fabled lights of Reason seem'd like torch-flames tost
　　　and driven—

All its music was as discord to the melody of heaven.

As I knelt and gazed (esteeming all the world beside but
　　　loss)

On the one lone star that glimmer'd o'er my Saviour's
　　　silent cross.

Brother, brother, canst thou wonder that, when peace began
　　　to brood

Over those wild troubled waters of my spirit's solitude,

I should turn and bless the angel who had shown that light
　　　divine ?

Blessing, see her—seeing, love her—win and bind her heart
　　　to mine ?

Shall I tell thee of the beauty of her sylph-like form and face,

Such as sculptor's hands, entranced all the while, might
　　　love to trace ?

Of her soft dark tresses shading the swift blushes of her
　　　cheek ?

Of her clear and thoughtful forehead, sunlit like a cloudland
　　　peak ?

Of her gentle heaving bosom, heaving o'er her passionate
    heart?

Of her soft blue eye that bound thee without thinking,
    without art—

But within whose cool deep fountain slept a thousand sunny
    rays?—

Tush! the world saw that, and often spoke thereof in heart-
    less praise.

No, I will not tell thee, brother, if I could for grief and
    tears—

Love is silent as the stars that love us in their voiceless
    spheres.

Thus far only—she was ever, as she wander'd by my side, .

Like a rill of spirit-music flowing with ethereal tide

Through my heart of hearts, and chasing all the discords
    lingering yet

On the ruffled waves of life that could not in an hour
    forget.

What, if on my holiest moments burst detested thoughts and
    vile,

Like a breath the cloud was scatter'd with the magic of her
    smile.

                                    c

Soon we parted—but that radiance pass'd not into mist or
    dreams,
Haunting still deep mystic caverns with the light of moon-
    light streams :
Yes, we parted—but that music did not die upon mine ears,
For its cycle hath no boundary, and its[3] lordliness no peers.
Thrice we met and thrice were sever'd, this the last sad fare-
    well sound
Ere earth's links should bind, we whisper'd, those Heaven
    had already bound.

'Twas a night of clouds and tempests sweeping through the
    void of black,
Every sad blast through the forest given in sadder echoes
    back,
Till they died among the cloisters with a melancholy cry
As of restless moaning waters or dark spectres hurrying by.
And dear thoughts would rise within me with their weeping
    train of woes,
But I shut my heart upon them, chased them ever as they rose,

[3] " Listening the lordly music flowing on
    The illimitable years."—TENNYSON'S *Ode to Memory.*

Rambled on through fancy labyrinths, dreaming o'er my
    Adeline,

Threw me on my couch, and sleeping still dreamt on that
    dream divine.

And I thought she look'd upon me with her own untroubled
    gaze,

Blushing while my silent rapture praised as language could
    not praise :

But beneath my eye her beauty grew to deepness more
    intense,

All that could be earthly melting into heavenlier innocence.

Brother,—*Sleep hath eyes*—and silence hears strange sounds
    at midnight hours,

Wonder then unbars the caverns of her phantom-haunted
    towers,

And we see prophetic visions—but, oh! never till that time

Saw I with my earnest eyes the secrets of night's lonely
    chime.

At her beauty I was troubled, so unearthly bright, and
    deep,

And I felt a cold misgiving stealing through my feverish
    sleep.

Brother, list! my dreams were startled; in my couch I sate
upright;

And I wildly gazed around me—not a star was in the
night,

But a mild and chasten'd radiance softly streaming fill'd my
room,

Centr'ing round her angel figure—even in death my light in
gloom.

Yes, she stood there—from her eye the tears fell silently and
fast;

If ye will, fond human frailty still victorious to the last:

Tears—aye well she knew the iron soon would rive this
quivering heart:

Tears—her home was far away, and I an exile, we must
part.

But methinks I could have borne far easier bosom-rending
groans

Than that mournful boding silence, and I cried in passionate
tones,

"Am I dreaming? oh, beloved, gaze I on thee there awake?

"Wherefore weepest thou? Speak—speak, for soon this
bursting heart will break!

" Hast thou left me then for ever, here upon this desolate
    shore ?

" Thou my only fellow-pilgrim—speak, speak, art thou
    mine no more ?"

And she spoke—her voice was music, music over waters
    heard,

The deep waters of that grief that in her bosom's depths
    was stirr'd.

" Yes, mine own one, we are parted, such as time and space
    can part—

" But for ever and for ever we are one in soul and heart:

" This shall seal me thine "—and speaking nearer to my side
    she press'd,

Till the bright apparel brush'd me flowing o'er her angel
    breast.

Words may never tell my rapture, blent with awe serenely
    proud,

As I felt her presence bending o'er me like a golden
    cloud;

As a moment on my bosom beat responsively her own,

As her lips touch'd mine—and in a moment I was there—
    alone.

Nothing saw I but the midnight's funeral blackness in my
    room,

Nothing heard I but the wind and raindrops driving through
    the gloom :

All my being, that had lately bloom'd with flowers and
    teem'd with springs,

Seem'd one dreary vast 'alone,' a barren wilderness of things.

Aye alone—the spell of sunshine that had fallen on my
    track,

Now was far beyond the clouds, its native sky had call'd it
    back :

I was left o'er moor and mountain still to wander wearily,

And the dead leaves round me telling, Autumn had come
    soon for me.

Endless seem'd the hours of darkness, yet they wore at last
    away,

And the morning dawn'd, though morning, still to me a
    midnight day.

She was dead, I knew more surely than if I had seen her die,

But grief clings to fragile anchors when the storms are
    hurtling by.

So at morning set I forth my heartless hopeless way to
    wend,

Sorrow clinging round my journey, sorrow brooding at the
    end.

But one met me, and he wept—I knew his tale ere he
    begun—

She had died at yester-midnight, dying as the bell peal'd
    ' one' !

Heavy-hearted I return'd—I could not bear her corse to
    see

Whom I just had seen apparell'd like one of the far countree.

Yes, I felt my heart was broken ! though for years it did
    not die,

But it must be with its treasure up in yon eternal sky,

God, my Father, He was there—my blessed Saviour, 'twas
    His home,

Adeline, and she who bore me harbour'd there, no more to
    roam.

And my earthly path was clouded, all its lingering gleams
    had fled,

Save the memories of communion with the living and the
    dead.

Oh, they sicken'd not, nor faded into fond imaginings,

For true joys, if only true, immortal are 'mid mortal
things:

Whilome they were golden lamps that o'er our pilgrim
pathway shone,

Whose dear light we fondly bless'd, and wended unrepining
on:

And when number'd with the past they sank not in the
misty sea

With the foul and base-born glimmer of the world's false-
hearted glee,

But majestically rose, an apotheosis of light,

Till they clomb the dark blue heavens, stars for ever 'mid
the night:

And thence shining on our pathway from their glorious
home afar,

Tell us of the things that have been, that they shall be, and
they are.

Brother, I have told thee all my gloomy tale of fear and
sin;

Ah, forgive me, for I could not die and keep it pent
within—

Since she went, this heart's beloved, thirteen dreary years
    have pass'd,
Something tells me in my bosom, this—joy, joy!—shall be
    my last.
Brother, I have lived and roam'd in tracking those I once
    beguiled,
To essay with me sin's fearful dark interminable wild;
Days and nights of supplication I have agonized for them,
Till to all, 'mid storm and shipwreck, beam'd the Star of
    Bethlehem.

Nothing now remains for lifetime—take my last, my fond
    farewell;
If a heart like mine can bless, Heaven bless thee more than
    heart can tell!
Grant that all my dark experience may be imaged back in light,
When reflected from the sunny waters of thy spirit bright:
Till thy race on earth is finish'd, and ye hasten to complete
Those our mother's vision saw, a blessed band at Jesus' feet.
And when I am dead, dear brother, lay me by the sacred yew
That o'ershades this heart's beloved. Fare thee well—adieu
    —adieu.

Trinity College, 1845.

THE THINGS THAT ARE.

"Ὅ ἐστιν ὂν ὄντως.

THE closing of a stormy night :—the wrecks
Of many tempests stranded on the shore
Of Time's mysterious sea :—and yet no break,
No far blue vista in the storm-tost drifts
Of clouds, that gather blackness ever and aye
Close round the wild horizon.   If a star
With trembling light, and that the light of tears,
Gleams for a moment through the vault of gloom,
The swift clouds, envying Hope's sweet messenger,
Quick shifting dim its radiance, and the void
Of darkness reigns supreme.   Perchance, anon,
A meteor with its dazzling train shoots by,
And hurries into nothingness—a dream
Of dying human glory—a bright torch

To light ambition to its starless tomb.

Once more the eye looks up, as if in fear

Of that which shall be, for the lightnings now

Are all abroad upon the winds of night,

Writing in vivid characters of flame,

Truths words might never utter, truths intense,

Of man's strange destiny and future worlds

Prophetic : brief their tale, as it is bright ;

And after them, dim thunder sounds far off,

Like waters, or the wail of nations come,

From the lone caverns of chill shadowy mountains,

In fitful bursts upon the startled ear.

All speak of woes and tempests past and coming. . . .

Is such the sky that stretches o'er the world ?

Fool, fool,—it cannot be—just close thine eye

And open it anew, and o'er its sweep

Will rise, in faëry pageantries of joy,

Life-pictures diverse far : young pleasure's train,

Dances, and revelries, and reckless smiles,

All cluster'd there beneath a cloudless sky :—

None know it is but painted o'er their heads,

And that the true dread heavens roll rife with storms.

Tush, tush, bend down thine ear and list again :

I listen'd, and the dulcet voice of song,

And music manifold of various spells,

And the yet sweeter tones of flattering hope,

Whispering of peace and pleasures without fail,

Smiled at my fears, and ask'd me tauntingly,

If I too smiled not.   But a deeper voice

Like that of thunder, utter'd answer—*Peace !*

There is no peace, and echoed still—*no peace :*

And all the after sounds of mirth, that came

Upon the moaning breezes, ever seem'd

To sicken on my weary soul, like things

Of little moment to a dying man.

Hast thou not often at lone hours of midnight,

When the vain troublous world is still, and thou

Art there amidst the universe alone,

Alone with visions of the vast unseen,

In the stern grandeur of eternal truth

Looming around thee, turn'd thy spirit's eye

Inward upon itself, and in a tone

Tremulous for fear of answer unforeseen,
Ask'd thyself what thy being's being is?
Aye, what that strange mysterious thing *self* is?
And all things seem to fall from off thee, like
The leaves of autumn, and the earth to sink,
The stars to fade, and all things be as dreams.
Oh! then the solitude of solitudes,
The feeling of unutter'd weariness,
Like shipwreck'd mariner cast far adrift
Upon a desert ocean, with its void
Crushes the heart: the spirit faints: till soon
The stern conviction that thou canst not stay
Heartless, and homeless, and companionless,
That struggle unto death thou must for life,
Floods all thy soul; and with a sudden spring
Of blended fear, and hope, and confidence,
Thou castest all that storm-tost thing, thyself,
Upon the blessed certainty of God:
And clingest unto Him, with energies
Lent by despair—the only anchor left;
If that could fail, all others were but straws.
Yet, clinging there, a voice within thee tells,

That cannot fail thee: 'tis thy Father's hand.
Poor child, He loves thee: love can never fail.
And then all grows serene like light, and Peace
Comes stealing o'er the waters, and aloft
Faith rises, Phœnix-like, amid the wreck.

So when that mystic undertone, *no peace,*
Like the dull clangour of a muffled bell
Rousing the sleep of a beleaguer'd town,
First mingled with those revelries of song,
Louder and louder pealing (whether they
Wax'd fainter, or its tone the clearer grew),
Until I seem'd to hear nor lyre nor dance,
But only that prophetic wailing; then
My spirit lost all consciousness of earth,
And listlessly I counted as they fell
The beatings of the heavy clock of Time.
I saw and slept, and sleeping still I heard;
And in my sleep my lips re-echoed ever
After that mighty pendulum of Fate
Words that it utter'd palpably,—*now*—*then :*
And *then* still follow'd *now,* and still the *now*

Preceded *then*, eternally the same.
Save when at intervals of mystic length,
The hours of those illimitable ages,
I heard a hammer strike some viewless sphere ;
And straightway through the universe of worlds,
In varying number but in tone the same,
Peal'd forth the everlasting answer, '*gone.*'

And is there nothing then that fleets not thus ?
Unconsciously I murmur'd.   At the words,
Came crowding on my spirit's inward eye
A thousand sunny visions—mine heart leapt
To welcome them—for there were cloudless scenes
Of childhood's happy rambles; there were thoughts
That blended with the burning dreams of youth,
And like the sunbeams to the sun flew back
As to their early home, where gushes ever
That fount within a fountain, human love;
When music held her calm unruffled spell,
Or trembled into sorrow, or did wail
With deepest spirit storms, and these again
Did soothe to rest in wondrous magic wise.

Childhood and youth rose thus, and thus laid out
Their rosy landscapes at my feet: I look'd
Once more,—once more,—a moment they were gone.
I could have wept, their sojourn was so brief;
But ere the tear fell from my eye, behold
New thoughts, new burning feelings, new desires
Came rushing o'er me: all the streams of love
From that young crystal fountain, music-like,
Flow'd a majestic river through the vale
Of life; and I was wandering by its banks,
And often paused my footstep, often gazed
Into what seem'd a nether sky, where heaven
With its unfathomable mysteries,
In characters of soften'd loveliness,
Was imaged in the watery mirror.   Oh
I could have linger'd by that stream, methought,
For ever and for ever, but its flow
Grew faint and fainter still, till all was air,
And viewless winds, and unremaining dreams.
Yes, I might tell for hours what there and then
Arose and vanish'd, till my bosom ached
And all my heart was pain'd within me: friends

They were and brothers, those light spirit-scenes,
For a few passing moments; but oh, when
My heart was going out towards them, when
Like bright homes nestling in a vale they seem'd
Where I long while might linger, as I mused,
Their cloud foundations sway'd before the wind;
For they were built upon the mists and winds,
And perishable were, and brief as they.

As one, awaking from a glorious train
Of dreams and phantasies at dead of night,
Looks forth upon the darkness for awhile,
Musing aghast; as if he thought straightway
Another image, beautiful as those
That have pass'd by him in their loveliness,
Would rise and fill the void of gasping thought:
But when the listless moments steal away
Unvision'd all and dreamless, doth start up
And question of himself what forms they were?
And what he is, and where, and whence, and how?
So I, as panting to lay hold on that
Which would not vanish at my touch like snow,

Struggled to cast myself from out myself
In secret prayer and agony of soul ;
And though in darkness, onward felt my way,
If haply I might find a rock whereon
To stay my weary foot ; for all that once
I deem'd substantial, had proved light as air,
And fragile as the foam on slippery waves.
The fashions of this world, its feasts and songs,
To my incredulous gaze seem'd planted now
Upon the words—*no peace.*   The course of Time,
Its seeming endless cycles, its vast spans,
Stretching like new horizons day by day
Before a journeying traveller, reaching far
Athwart the clouded Past and clouded Future,
In countless maze of circles, as I gazed,
All rested on one shifting sliding point,
Which men call Present, which was ever gone
Though still renew'd like shower drops in a stream.
And when with sickening soul I turn'd away
From all the unrealities of earth,
And the brief phantoms of historic worlds,
To what I deem'd were everlasting things,

And truths that borrow'd immortality
Of deeper things than mortal hand might touch
And mortal foot explore ; lo, these likewise
Had vanish'd : darkness wrapt my steps in gloom.
Yet there are things that in the darkness live
A life intense and vivid as in light.
Prayer then can wrestle on victoriously,
And Faith without suspicion lean her hand
Upon a viewless anchor : there is One
To whom the night translucent seems as day,
And though unseen, I felt His presence filling
The vast and vacant chambers of my soul.
And one by one, as wrapt in silvery mist
That caught their diamond brightness, like the stars
Of twilight visiting a lonely vale,
The words of promise beauteously brake forth
And kindled into radiance.   For awhile
Wonder and rapture reft my soul of thought,
And left me tranced as a child who first
Stands on the shore of blue phosphoric waves
At midnight : but ere long the dews of heaven
Shed balm upon my fever'd spirit : all

Was peace : and the pure atmosphere of truth
Around me, like an infant's holy dream,
Diffused a light and beauty all its own.
Ah ! words can never tell my bliss, for I
Had found what my soul long'd for ; I had found
My spirit's home, my Father's presence, found
Wherewith to sate my bosom's infinite ;
And He was smiling on me, and His peace
Was in my heart of hearts, that peace divine
Which passes understanding.   I did weep,
But they were tears of joy : I sigh'd, but 'twas
The fulness of a heart, that overflow'd
Nor otherwise could utter what within
Was hidden.   Long my musing lasted : long
I held intense communion with my God.

Oh, hast thou known the yearnings of delight
It is to commune with a tender father,
To cast the burden of a host of cares
Upon his father-heart, to feel thyself
His child, and in that blessed privilege
To ask his sympathy, his care, his love,

And with a deep familiar earnestness
Blend all thy thoughts with his, with filial fear
Yet fearless in affection ?   If thou hast
Thou knowest an emblem, faint indeed and dim,
But yet the brightest, loveliest earth affords
Of the joy fountains gushing in the heart
Of one, who, from the world a fugitive,
And from despair, and darkness, and thick doubt,
Finds there is yet one bosom where to cast
His sorrows, and a Father's heart that glows
For him, and yearns to greet him as a child.
Entranced, imparadised in joy, I knelt
There at the footstool of my Father's throne,
My Father's and my God's, and from His smile
Drank life, drank beauty, drank intensest love,
From love, and life, and beauty's fountain-head.
I may not tell ye more ; but when that dream
Of glory (if ye reckon those things dreams
That have a deep and vast reality
Beyond all certainties of sight and sense,
As reaching the unseen eternal world)
Had pass'd me, like a golden sunset cloud,

My soul was as a sea of light, whereon
No grief did cast a shadow; such as oft
Thou mayst have seen within a summer sky,
Sleeping untroubled in calm mellow light,
Above the spot where the sun's chariot wheels
Sank slowly into ocean. Yes, it pass'd,
But yet I felt it was my own for ever,
A wealth, a rapture, an inheritance.
And quickly I bethought me once again
Of all those airy scenes of young delight,
That whilome, as I gazed, had pass'd away,
Or seem'd to pass, like phantom soulless things.
And a voice spake within me, " Thou hast found,
By finding out thy spirit's home in God,
A master key of truth that shall unlock
The thousand wards of earthly mysteries ;
And show thee unto whom alone, the good,
The true, the noble, pure, and beautiful,
Whatever seems to mortals loveliest,
Can have or claim an immortality
Of goodness, truth, or beauty—'tis to those
Whose hearts are right, whose beings one with God,

Who in Him find their all: to other men,

The beauteous things that pass them by on earth,

Oh, yes, they are immortal, but it is

An immortality of deathless woe,

That haunts them with the sting of lost delight."

And once again, retracing all my steps,

I gazed upon those lovely scenes of life;

Those passion fountains of unfathom'd depth,

Those springs of human love, those beautiful homes

Of friendship and affection, which the dove

Of Peace broods over evermore, and there

Doth shelter underneath her sacred wing

A father's heart, a mother's, or a child's,

Those dearest types of heaven; and lo, they rose

In tenfold loveliness before me, rose

More passionately beautiful than ever;

And oh, the blessed change!—they vanish'd not.

At first my faithless heart grew chill with fear,

And trembled as the moments swift flew by,

And the far beatings of the clock of time

Again struck dimly on mine ear, but soon

Faith whisper'd, " They are amaranthine now,
Thou livest now 'mid everlasting things—
Fear not: what once was of the present, soon
Is number'd with the past: what once was *now*,
Let one brief moment pass away, is *then:*
And Time may count these hours and cycles, gone,
But Faith hath vanquish'd Time: and she beholds
The things that have been, being, and to be."

In peace, my spirit linger'd on the scenes
Of her eternal Past:—in peace I mused
On those delicious spots of earth, those fair
Oases in the wilderness of life,
Those isles too often few and far between,
Emblems of home upon the homeless sea,
Those Edens blooming in a ruin'd world,
Those sunbeams 'mid the storm-clouds all astray,
Those gushing springs within a thirsty land,
Those stars that startle us like friends at night,
Those blessed things so inexpressibly dear,
There, there I mused—there wander'd like a child
Through flowerets all his own; and when at length

The cycle was complete, and through the heavens
Thrice peal'd the everlasting answer, Gone,
I look'd upon those scenes of far delight,
And there unfading and unchanged they lay
In the clear cloudless region of the Past,
Imperishably shrined in love and light.

Trinity College, 1845.

SAMSON.

*[The story of Samson is put into the mouth of Manoah, who relates it
to his attendant shortly before his death.]*

"Ibi demum morte quievit."

VIRGIL. *Æneid.* ix. 445.

GIVE me thy hand, brave stripling, for mine eyes
Are dim with age and many sorrows : rise
And lead me to that rocky seat, whereon
Beams the full radiance of the summer sun ;
And basking in his glory, ere he laves
His chariot wheels in yonder western waves,—
Again my frozen life-streams onward flowing,
Again my heart with manhood's pulses glowing,—
I'll grant thy eager and long-sought request,
Before I sink to silence and to rest.

Yes, thou hast urged me oftentimes to tell
How my child Samson lived and fought and fell;
By all the silent pleading of those years
Spent with an old man in this vale of tears,
By all the brooding thunder-clouds of war
Skirting the confines of our land afar,
And by thy hopes to light the latent fire
Of thy young heart at Samson's funeral pyre;
I felt thy silent longings; but my heart,
Though school'd in grief, refused the mourner's part:
I could not tell thee without tears his story—
I could not weep o'er Samson's tomb of glory:—
But now I feel, I know my hour is nigh.
Who weeps with heaven before him? fix thine eye
On mine: the sun shines cloudless: it is well:
Now listen to an old man's tale, and tell
The after centuries when I am gone,
So spake Manoah of his only son.

Yes, the dark clouds are breaking from my sight,
My childhood floats before me: bathed in light

Again I see my fond parental home
Smiling in beauty, and again I roam
Its green and quiet pastures.   Like a dream
Flow'd on apace with me life's early stream,
And roughen'd as it flow'd : for vengeance fell
On guilty and apostate Israel[1].
And we, who sate beneath our household vine,
Fled for long years before the Philistine,
And groan'd to see the spoiler's ruthless hand
Crush the fair promise of our holy land.

Then was it, in that dark and cloudy day
When Israel wander'd shepherdless astray,
That first I saw the partner of my life,
And sought her hand, and she became my wife.
No festal banquet graced our nuptial eve,
No virgins, chaplet-crown'd, came forth to weave
The dance before us, or with sacred hymn
Tended us home :—but on the mountains dim,

---

[1] " The children of Israel did evil again in the sight of the Lord ; and the Lord delivered them into the hands of the Philistines forty years."— Judg. xiii. 1.

In silence and in solitude at night,

Our parents ratified the solemn rite.

They call'd the stars to witness, and the rills

Made answer to the everlasting hills—

Espousals meet for Samson's parents! years

Of brief tranquillity, and many tears

Pass'd silently. But Heaven who gave the bride

The pledge of bridal blessedness denied;

My wife was barren and bare not[2]: alas,

Too oft I saw the cloud of anguish pass

Across her lovely brow, and often read,

Albeit not a whisper'd word she said,

The passionate prayer of Rachel in her eye,

" My husband, give me children, or I die[3]."

The foe was seeking other fields of prey;

Our home began to smile anew; the day

Was wearing into twilight; when I heard

My wife's quick footstep on the verdant sward.

---

[2] "And his wife was barren, and bare not."—Judg. xiii. 2.

[3] Gen. xxx. 1.

" Manoah," with excited joy she spake,

"At thy command by yonder wooded brake

" I watch'd the flock, and on the fountain's stone

" Was seated, musing as I deem'd alone,

" When on a sudden I was made aware

" That some one stood beside me ;—without care,

" Deeming thou needest me, my eyes I raised,

" And on the messenger unconscious gazed :

" But when I saw him I was troubled :—white

" Was his apparel as transparent light,

" And, like the visions of prophetic trance,

" The awful beauty of his countenance.

" My heart misgave me :—was he from above ?—

" But fear and wonder both were lost in love

" When from his lips the blessed tidings fell

" Of bliss to me, and hope to Israel :—

" ' Lo, thou art barren, and thou bearest not ;

" ' Woman, bewail no more thy childless lot :

" ' Behold thou shalt conceive and bear a child,

" ' A Nazarite devoted, undefiled,

" ' Who while his holy hair unrazor'd grows

" ' Shall save his people from their taunting foes.' "

And as in thought she drank the promised cup
Of motherly endearment, love lit up
Her face with pure delight; she could not weep
Though tears were in her eyes, but all the deep
Expressions of a wife's, a woman's soul
Over her face in crimson blushes stole.

Faith wrestled in my heart, and won. I felt
That God had spoken to her, and we knelt
Together suppliant before His throne
And made our soul's harmonious longings known.
So ever used we, and though often cast
As exiles on the desert's howling waste,
Or nightly lurking where the secret wave
Murmur'd but shone not in the starless cave,
Or kneeling on our fathers' burial sod,
One utterance told our yearning thoughts to God.

We pray'd, "O Lord, parental wisdom, grant."
He heard us; and the heavenly visitant
As she was seated in the lonely field
Again his glory and his grace reveal'd.

Straightway she ran and call'd me; love divine
Shone calmly in his human eye benign,
And when I ask'd him of our promised child,
How we should train him for the Lord, he smiled
And spake so graciously that I began
To feel towards him as a brother man.
He only veil'd his brightness—when I pray'd
That he would tarry where the grateful shade
Fell on the glebe from some o'erhanging rock,
The while I brought a firstling from my flock,
He answer'd, "If a firstling thou wilt bring,
"Then offer to the Lord thine offering."
And when astonish'd I besought his name,
He still repress'd my boldness[4].   Soon the flame
Is kindled, and the victim's life-blood flows,
And sweet perfumes of sacrifice arose ;
But as they wreath'd towards the azure sky,
Behold the angel of the Lord drew nigh,
And slowly rising with the incense-cloud
Flame-like ascended up to heaven. We bow'd

---

[4] Judg. xiii. 18: "Seeing it is SECRET;" *margin,* "WONDERFUL."
Cf. Isa. ix. 6.

Our faces to the earth on bended knee,

And trembled at the sight exceedingly ;

For when I saw the fiery track he trod,

This is, methought, none other than that God

Who spake to Noah and to Abraham,

And said to Moses, " I am that I am ;"

Who led our fathers through the ocean deeps,

Which stood at His command in rock-like heaps[5];

Who wrapt in clouds of darkness and of storm

Rent Sinai's cliffs before His viewless form ;—

And could He our presumptive eye forgive,

Who[6] threaten'd " None shall see My face and live"?

But then my wife's unwavering faith subdued

My struggling spirit's dark disquietude:

I could not tremble, when I look'd on her,

The mother of our land's deliverer:

And still I see in memory's vista now

The calm affiance of her cloudless brow.

[5] " The floods stood upright as an heap."—Exod. xv. 8.
[6] Exod. xxxiii. 20.

And dost thou ask me who it was that came,
And rose celestial in that altar flame?
I shall behold Him, but not now—the Seed
Who, woman-born, shall bruise the serpent's head;
He whom the dying patriarch divine
Foretold should come of Judah's royal line;
Whom Balaam saw in vision from afar,
Israel's bright sceptre, Jacob's morning star:
Who dawning on this world of wreck and crime
In the ripe fulness of predestined time,
Not with such transitory beams of light
As only greet some favour'd prophet's sight,
But born albeit of no mortal birth,
Shall stand incarnate God upon the earth.

The old man paused awhile—his silent gaze
Seem'd rapt in far hopes of the latter days,
And mute his ear, as though the evening breeze
Grew vocal with angelic melodies,
The echo of that everlasting song
Which swells through all creation. But ere long

Back, as athirst for sympathy, he brought
His spirit from that glowing world of thought,
And with a deeper mellowness of tone,
As though communing with himself, spake on.

My child, my child, my loved and only son!
I weep not for thee, Samson: thou art one
Of that great army of the living God,
Who militant by faith to glory trod;
Who out of weakness valiant wax'd in fight,
And singly turn'd the alien camps to flight:
Still march they on, a mighty victor host
Whose foremost ranks the stream of death have cross'd,
And calmly resting, where the wicked cease
From troubling and the weary are at peace,
Await in bliss expectant, till the last
Lone band of faithful ones hath safely pass'd.
Enough for me, my Samson in his day
Bare a bright standard 'mid that vast array,
And heard, I doubt not, when his race was run,—
" Servant and soldier of the Lord, well done!"

I weep not for my child—I knew his star
Had mark'd him for the stormy ranks of war,
And read his future, when he lay at rest
A folded blossom on his mother's breast;
Who often bade me note his strength of limb,
And fondly ask'd, "Was ever babe like him?"
And when in after years upon my knee
He sate in childhood's playful prattling glee,
Still would he ask with beaming eye and face,
"Tell me some story of our fathers' race."
But chief my words his mute attention caught,
What time I told how God for Israel fought,
When underneath the silent strokes of prayer
Proud Amalek was smitten with despair,
When Canaan's banded armies fled amain
Routed and ruin'd on Megiddo's plain,
When Deborah awoke her pæan song,
And Barak captive led captivity along.
But when I told how mighty Gideon rose
And saved our bleeding country from her foes,
Fronting the hosts of darkness and of death,
Clad in the panoply of prayer and faith

Invincible—it seem'd as though my child
Had found a kindred spirit—sternly he smiled,
And shook, as shakes the storm dark ocean's froth,
His unshorn locks in sign of kindling wrath,
And ask'd impatient if the hour drew nigh,
When he might likewise rush to strife and victory.

The Lord Jehovah bless'd him : and he grew,
As grows the lordly cedar, fed with dew
From heaven, and nourish'd by the early sun,
Upon the snowy peaks of Lebanon :
Soon swept the wild blasts o'er him, and the cloud
Of thunder and of storm his branches bow'd ;
In vain—for, laughing at their idle shocks,
His strength was in the everlasting rocks :
And when bereft, beleaguer'd, and betray'd,
At length he fell, his vast and ruining[7] shade
Its crushing devastation scatter'd wide
On Philistina in her hour of pride.

[7] "Heaven *ruining* from heaven."
                    Par. Lost, vi. 868.

The Lord Jehovah bless'd him : few could brook
Of friends or foes, his calm defiant look,
And, though to us all grace and gentleness,
Few the high conflicts of his soul could guess.
Oh, how his mother loved him, how he loved
His angel mother !—I have seen him moved
To tears, whenever by our lonely hearth
She told the awful secret of his birth,
And with her folded hands besought that he
Might never shame his glorious destiny,
But without lingering thought of home or her
Be unto death our land's deliverer.

Years glided on apace ;—with holy awe
His ripening strength we noted, and we saw
At times a lofty grandeur in his mien
Of high emprize, so tranquilly serene,
That told no human impulse moved his soul
Obedient[s].   Under that divine control,

---

[s] "The Spirit of the Lord began to move him at times in the camp
of Dan."—Judg. xiii. 25.

Upon the mountain heights companionless,
Or in the waste and howling wilderness,
Far off he wander'd, meditative, lone,
Musing stern deeds of vengeance all his own,
Or, burning with impatient hopes, began
To join his comrades in the camp of Dan.

Alas, he found no breast amid his peers
That shared his thoughts of glory. Crush'd by years
Of craven flight, or grinding servitude,
The lion heart of Israel was subdued,
All save his own unconquerable will,
That wrestled on in prayer and trusted still.

Alone he went to Timnath, inly driven—
But mark how fathomless the ways of Heaven!
There, as he lurk'd amid the laden vines,
He saw a daughter of the Philistines,
A virgin fair as light to look upon,
Who wander'd in the careless evening. One
She was, who, born of that accursed stock,
Grew as a heath-flower on the barren rock.

And Samson's spirit clave to hers ;—but when
He sought impetuously our home again,
And told us of her alien race and name,
The full heart of his mother glow'd with shame,
And sternly spake she :—" Is there never one
" Of all the daughters of our kin, my son,
" Not one with whom in wedlock thou couldst dwell
" Of all the far-famed maids of Israel,
" That thou hast chosen out a stranger bride
" From our uncircumcised foes ? "   He sigh'd,
And look'd to heaven in silence ; not a shade
Of earthly passion on his dark cheek play'd,
But hopes of battle and of victory
Wrought in his soul and kindled in his eye,
Till, as he turn'd and look'd on us and smiled,
The parents' spirit quail'd before their child ;
Or rather in that Presence he adored,
Though then we knew not, all was of the Lord.

I know it now, I know it : thou hast seen
The planets glide along their path serene,

SAMSON.

Diffusing softly their benignant light
Over the stillness of the summer night,
While steals from every pendant orb of gold
The music of their silence,—when behold
A meteor, with its dark forebodings blent,
Flames far athwart the troubled firmament,
And to the feeble ken of mortals mars
The changeless march and order of the stars;
But both, methinks, to His omniscient eye,
Who scans the cycles of eternity,
Pursue their destined path, and both fulfil
The fiat of His everlasting will.

And such was Samson's mission, as I deem'd,
Which then so dark and so mysterious seem'd,
For God was with him; wheresoe'er he press'd,
His spirit moved him, and His presence bless'd.
Bear witness, Timnath, when on love intent
A lion like a kid unarm'd he rent,
And from its swarming carcase subtly wrought
That deadly and disastrous riddle, fraught

With woe. Bear witness, widow'd Askelon,

Reft of thy children, God was with my son.

Bear witness, Etham's cloud-engirdled crest,

Where eagle-like he built his rocky nest

Aloft, alone, with God communing there

In solitary thought and secret prayer.

Bear witness of that hour, Philistia, when

Besieged by foes and faithless countrymen,

Arm'd only with the jaw-bone of an ass,

He fell'd thy choicest warriors like the grass,

And smote through brazen helms and plated mail

A thousand men in Ramath-Lehi's vale:

And when his spirit fail'd at eventide

Drank from the heaven-sent "well of him that cried[9]."

Yes, God the Lord was with him. His the might,

That braced his soul and nerved his arm in fight;

And His the fountain of exhaustless thought

That flow'd from Samson's rugged lips untaught,

---

[9] "He called the name thereof Enhakkore;" *margin*, "the well of him that cried."—Judg. xv. 19.

When, at his bidding, with obedient feet,
All Israel throng'd around his judgment-seat.

Then all men call'd us blessed : peace again
Shed its rich plenty over hill and plain ;
The fields were white with flocks ; and, loved of God,
Again our land with milk and honey flow'd ;
Age in his presence bow'd, and virgins young
With tabrets and with dance his triumphs sung,
And parents taught their infants' lips to frame
Their first fond blessings on our Samson's name.
A few short years of mirth and minstrelsy,
And, oh, the harrowing change to mine and me !
Our foes again victorious ; and our child
Begirt by hatred, and by love beguiled,
Shorn of his Godlike strength, bereaved of sight
And freedom, in the dungeon's loathsome night,
The slave of slaves who mock'd his every sigh,
And sported with his only prayer—to die.
Woe for his mother, woe ! the tidings crush'd
Her heart:—when forth companionless he rush'd

Singly a thousand warriors to assail,

I never saw her glowing cheek turn pale ;

But when she heard upon that awful night,

" Thy Samson is no more a Nazarite,"

Long while she sate in speechless anguish there,

A mute and marble likeness of despair,

Till from her breaking heart these words found way,

" My God...." she struggled, but she could not pray—

" My husband"—and she shook in every limb,

" He hath abandon'd God, and God abandon'd him."

But why retrace the story of his fall,—

Alas, too well, too widely known by all?

Delilah's arts ;—his weakness warn'd in vain,

Thrice warn'd, thrice yielding to the slavish chain

Of venal Beauty's lying blandishment,

And still entangled when the snare was rent;—

That fatal couch;—that dark perfidious hour

When he betray'd his citadel of power:

The quenching of those eyes in endless night

No foe had ever dared to meet in fight;

The fetters forged his freeborn limbs around;
The fetid prison where with slaves he ground;
And, worst of all, the shouts of high acclaim
Before him raised to Dagon's cursed name.—
Enough: I bless the Hand that smote him now,
And taught him though with bitter tears to bow,
Until he learnt beneath the chastening rod
That he was only strong, while strong in God.

Hark! there are sounds of revelry and mirth.
There is a feast to Dagon; and the earth
Rings with the shout exultingly again
Of that far-echoing sacrificial strain:
See, Gaza's eager population waits
The opening of those massive temple gates.
He comes! he comes! on his triumphal car,
Deck'd with the gorgeous pageantries of war,
Is rear'd the hideous idol; one and all
Before their god in low prostration fall.
And hark again, those wild and dissonant cries
In proud defiance swelling to the skies—

"Hail, Dagon! thou hast fought for us and won!

"Hail, Dagon, hail! Where lies Manoah's son?

"Where is the God of Israel? let Him now

"Avenge His cause; and be our champion thou!"

Again the gates are closed, again the din

Rings through the joyous city. But within

Dispersed through courts and crowded galleries,

Whose spacious roof receives the welcome breeze,

Behold, the choicest of Philistia's peers,

The bloom of all her beauty: echoing cheers

Peel through the temple of the idol god,

And wine and jesting fill the vast abode,

Till in their impious merriment they call

For Samson's feats to crown their festival.

Hark yet again, one universal cry,

A ruin'd nation's groan of agony,

With wailing fills the vast of heaven :—again,

The dying shrieks of thousands from that fane :.

Again—and Gaza holds her fearful breath,—

And all is mute as sleep, the sleep of death.

To Zorah's vale full soon the tidings sped,

Where lone I watch'd his mother's dying bed;

For ever since he fell Delilah's prey,

She like a flower had wither'd day by day,

Calm, tearless, uncomplaining, yet I knew

Her broken heart had found no healing dew.

But when her ear the hurried message caught,

That God deliverance by his death had wrought;

The banquet, and the shouts that rend the air,

His deeds of might, his last victorious prayer,

The pillars grasp'd and shaken to and fro,

The helpless agonizing cries of woe,

Until the temple's shatter'd roof and dome

Wrapt him and all in one terrific tomb;—

Then first a smile of glory on her cheek

Spoke of such bliss as language could not speak:

She raised her overflowing eyes to heaven,

And wept for joy, " My Samson is forgiven."

My tale is told—too soon the sepulchre

That closed o'er Samson was unseal'd for her;

And I was left my nation's peace to see—
Peace which my child had won, though not for me:
Farewell! our circle gathers in the sky,
And as they died in faith, so would I die.

Banningham, 1850.

NINEVEH.

"Opinionum commenta dies delet : naturæ judicia confirmat."

Cic. *de Nat. Deor.*

I.

Woe for the land of Asshur ! she who sate
   Queen of the nations, princess of the peers ;
How sits she as a widow desolate,
   In bitterness of soul and silent tears !
   Great Nineveh is fallen ! Pale with fears
She sits in her sepulchral greatness, hoary
   With lapse of unknown centuries of years ;
And strangers roam her haunts of sometime glory,
Deciphering with pain her once transparent story.

II.

Woe for the land of Asshur ! she who nursed
   The world's forefathers in her golden plains,
And cradled by her mighty streams the first
   Primeval race of heroes ! What remains

F

Of all her trophies and colossal fanes?
Stern, shapeless heaps of ruin, mouldering slow
    Beneath the fiery sun and torrent rains:—
Wild heedless hordes about her come and go:—
An unloved spectacle of unlamented woe.

III.

Woe for the land of Asshur!   Greece hath bow'd
    Her head beneath the chariot-wheels of Time;
But sorrow, like a distant mountain-cloud,
    Hath hung its lucid veil above her clime,
    And only made her virtues more sublime.
All centuries have wept her fall, and sung
    Her greatness and her grief in loftiest rhyme;
And, lingering still her haunted fanes among,
Repictured, from her age, her loveliness when young.

IV.

Woe for the land of Asshur!   Salem lies,—
    Salem, her former captive, lies in gloom;
And Zion, twice a widow, mourns and sighs,
    And lingers, spectre-like, beside the tomb

Of her first bridal blessedness and bloom.

She mourns, but mourns in hope; for God hath spoken

    The mystic number of her years of doom;

She waits the beacon-light, the Gospel token,

When stanch'd shall be her wounds, and all her chains be

    broken.

v.

But woe for thee, O Asshur! Few bemoan

    Thy giant desolations, void and vast;

No beauty smiles on thy sepulchral stone.

    The solitary stranger stands aghast

    At thee, but weeps not; and the fitful blast

Sighs in thy palaces. Nor canst thou borrow

    Far hopes to cheer the present and the past;

No dawn shall glimmer on thy night of sorrow,

Its silence and its sadness hath no bright to-morrow.

vi.

What though above thy solitudes the Spring

    Her fairy mantle ever throws anew;

Though smiles the early Summer, carpeting

    Thy wastes with flowers of scarlet and of blue,

F 2

And tangled labyrinths of every hue?

    To one who knew thee in thy prime it seems

        A sad heart's laughter, to itself untrue;

    A captive's reverie,—a widow's dreams,—

The bubbles breaking fast on dark and troubled streams.

VII.

    Where are thy frowning towers and scornful walls,

        And spacious parks, by hanging gardens spann'd?

    Where are thy regal palaces, whose halls

        Of sculptured alabaster proudly stand,

        The envy and the fame of every land,

Dyed purple and vermilion; echoing

        With bursts of song, by gales of fragrance fann'd;

Enrich'd with every great and gorgeous thing,—

Meet dwelling-place for thee, supreme Assyrian King?

VIII.

    Where is thy stern array of warrior sons,—

        The peerless maidens of Chaldea's bloom,—

    The laughter of her myriad little ones;—

        The voice of merchandise,—the mingled hum

Of citizens, and pilgrims who have come

   From far to view her greatness ;—the low sighs

   Of love,—the strains of music never dumb,—

The banquetings beneath her azure skies,

Or long luxurious dance of torch-light revelries ?

IX.

Where is the idol faith that once was hers,—

   The victims on her altars wont to bleed ?

Her temples, throng'd with prostrate worshippers,

   And guarded by that winged-lion breed—

   The awful symbols of a perish'd creed,

Whose forms of might their portals still defẽnd ;

   Whose wings betoken omnipresent speed ;

And brows of lofty human mould portend

The knowledge of the gods and wisdom without end ?

X.

Oh, weep for Nineveh !—the scorn or pity,

   From age to age, of every passer by.

" Is this," they ask [1], " the glad, rejoicing city,

   Who said,—' I am, and none beside me' ?   Why

[1] "This is the rejoicing city that dwelt carelessly, that said in her heart, I am, and there is none beside me : how is she become a desolation."—Zeph. ii. 15.

Doth she in wreck and desolation lie?"
Great Nineveh is fallen!   Transitory
   As slopes a meteor through the midnight sky;—
Who shall repaint her vanish'd scenes of glory,
Or weave her shatter'd woof of fragmentary story?

XI.

Though gorgeous fictions have been pass'd along
   The half-incredulous ages down to this,—
What boots it to relate, in idle song,
   How Ninus and divine Semiramis[2]
   First founded yonder vast metropolis;
And left a lineage of kings, whose names
   Stand tomb-like o'er oblivion's dark abyss,
Until, to hide his everlasting shames,
Sardanapalus lit his country's funeral flames?

XII.

Thus, o'er the keen blue night of northern climes
   A rose-blush, as of morning, seems to glow;
With waves of undulating light at times,
   And ruddy jets of flame that come and go,

   [2] See Dictionary of Biography, under Ninus.

And fitful meteors flashing to and fro,—

A dome of living splendours; but anon

Gloom settles on those silent wastes of snow;

The colours fade like dreams, and all is wan,

Save intermittent starlight, dimly glimmering on.

XIII.

Thus rose and sank those myths of by-gone ages:

Swiftly they sank, and darkness block'd my sight;

Till suddenly, from Inspiration's pages,

There flash'd a few and flickering beams of light

On distant fragments of Assyria's night.

So have I wander'd in some giant cave,

Whose sides of rock and pendent stalactite

Caught radiance from my torch, at times, and gave

A momentary brightness to some gushing wave.

XIV.

And first, far looming in the mist of years,

Stood Nimrod[3], mighty in the sight of God,—

Lord of the chase; before him earth appears

Strewn with the desolations of the flood,

---

[3] Gen. x. 8—11.

But limitless and lordless.   Forth he stood,
　First King of men, and, ranging in the free
　　Far forests with his teeming multitude,
　Where Tigris rolls to Persia's emerald sea,
Builded, for his great name, the infant Nineveh.

XV.

Thus clothed his form in brightness, and then fail'd
　The beam reflected from the sacred page;
And close, impenetrable darkness veil'd
　The long succeeding ages.   Age on age,
　　Basking in peace, or tost with warfare's rage,
They pass'd before my musing sight once more;
　Their voices did my lingering ear engage;
The hum of teeming myriads, like the roar
Of mighty waters chafing on an unseen shore.

XVI.

Long while I mused her story, how she grew
　Alone in greatness, and in guilt alone;
Until they left the God their fathers knew,
　And shadow'd forth the unseen Eternal One

In idol images of brass and stone.
(Fools! though the earth too mean a footstool were,
 The starry heavens for Him too base a throne)
Till God, at length, in wrath abandon'd her,
O her own lusts to be the slave and worshipper.

XVII.

In greatness and in wickedness she grew:
 Ambition's lurid and deceptive star
To distant lands her conquering armies drew,
 And fill'd her streets with sights and sounds of war,---
 The chariot and the glancing scimitar:
Debasing lust her native homes defiled
 With tears of hapless virgins brought from far:
Her heaps of gold insatiate avarice piled;
And pleasure, with young hopes, her votaries beguiled.

XVIII.

Thus great in glory, and too great in crime,
 The upland slope of fame she seem'd to tread;
And on from height to giddy height did climb,
 And fix'd her dwelling 'mid the stars, and said,

"No thunders there could scathe her lofty head."

Was there no voice her peril to proclaim,

 Ere her proud sons were number'd with the dead?

Hark! as I ponder'd o'er her shatter'd fame,

In rugged uncouth verse, the mystic answer came.

  Calmly glow'd the setting sun

  Upon the dark of Lebanon;

  Till, ere it sank, each cedar spire

  Was clad in a robe of golden fire,

  And a smile of light broke gloriously

  On the sullen waves of the Western sea.

  Far off, on Carmel's rocky fell,

  There sate the seer of Israel;

  He watch'd the dying gleams of day

  From tide and turret fade away,

  And deeply he sigh'd for the land of God,

  And inly murmur'd, "Ichabod."

  He look'd again, a flash of light

  On the far horizon's deepening night!

  Loth to quit so fair a clime,

  Hath the sun reversed the march of time?

Or is it the reflex glory cast

From mighty meteors streaming past?

His prophetic eye divine

More truly read that sacred sign:

He felt that a message from God was near,

And he bow'd his head in silent prayer.

"Go forth, go forth, thou prophet of the Lord

(Thus thrill'd his soul the penetrating word):

Against that great and guilty city cry,

Whose wickedness hath reach'd to heaven; for I,

The Lord Jehovah, have commission'd thee

A herald of my wrath to Nineveh."

A tempest shook the prophet's soul,

And trembling seized him past control.

Not the march through far-off lands,

Not the blasts of desert sands,

Not the taunts and proud despite

Of the godless Ninevite,

Not the wrathful threatenings

Of the Assyrian king of kings,

Not the leaguéd hosts of hell,

Moved the seer of Israel.

Yet shook he like a wind-tost oak to go

Proclaiming wrath and woe ;

For well he knew how mercy dwelt above,

And deeply had experienced "God is love[4]."

    *   *   *   *

Dark tempest on the waters : see, they rise

Faster and fiercer round that little bark !

Her mariners with agonizing cries

Betake them to their gods for aid, but dark

Still lay the tempest on the waters : dark

Grew every face, and darker grew the skies :

They strew'd the billows with their Tyrian wares,

  Redoubling their wild prayers.

Till lo, quoth one, " Yon strange and fearful man

Calmly hath slumber'd since the storm began.—

What meanest thou, O sleeper ! rise and call

 Upon thy God to bend His gracious ear,

 And think on us in pity, ere we all

  Together perish here."

         [4] Jonah iv. 2.

Then rose the prophet Jonah—calm his mien,

In its stern sadness awfully serene—

One glance he took upon the raging main,

Then slowly scann'd that trembling crew again.

His steady eye disturb'd them ; for the change

Wrought in his slumber seem'd unearthly strange.

Surely in that profound, mysterious dream

The Lord his God hath spoken unto him,

Who hitherto had ever seem'd to live

In terror, like a guilty fugitive,

But now, amid the storm stood forth alone

    The only fearless one.

" Who art thou ?" tremblingly they ask'd, " and what

Thy country and thy race ?"—He trembled not,

    But prophet-like replied :

" I am a Hebrew, and I bow the knee

To Him who made the heaven and earth and sea :

Fear not, but cast me in the raging tide,

Because for me yon raging billows roar,—

And peace shall tend you to your distant shore."

Oh, unexampled faith, unequall'd trust

Placed in his God by a frail child of dust !

Hosanna! from the caverns of the grave,

    Beneath the ocean wave,

Climbs to the throne of God through sea and air,

The voice of confidence and praise and prayer[5].

    Hell, who had gloried in the prophet's fall,

    And gloated o'er her coming carnival,

    Heard it and trembled—dark, mysterious sign[6]

    Of that predicted Conqueror Divine,

        Whose advent was the token

        Of chains and fetters broken,

    Who, buried like that seer beneath the earth,

    Should mar the triumph of her fiendish mirth,

    And wrest the ponderous keys of death away,

    And lead captivity his captive prey.

        *   *   *   *

It was the glow of eventide—behold

Upon his throne of ivory and gold,

Assyria's monarch proudly gazed around,

While prostrate kings before him kiss'd the ground.

    When lo! a messenger in haste is brought,

    His blanch'd cheeks with a tale of danger fraught :—

[5] Jonah's prayer, rising at its close to a song of praise, was uttered before his deliverance.—Jonah ii. 1—9.

[6] Matt. xii. 39—41.

" This livelong day," he falter'd, " there hath been
A prophet such as earth hath never seen,
From street to street who wanders sad and slow,
With one stern message of impending woe—
' Ere forty suns have risen on Nineveh,
' Her guilt and glory shall have ceased to be.' "

Straightway a smile of proud derision curl'd
The lip of that proud monarch of the world;
But, ere he spake, his courtiers crowded near,
    And pour'd into his ear,
What busy fame had spread from lip to lip,—
The story of that tempest-shatter'd ship,
And that unheard-of miracle, that bore
The Prophet Jonah to his destined shore.
Long while he grappled with his fears, and then
Look'd round his court in marvel; and again
He gazed upon those floods of radiance bright
Which bathed his palace in their golden light,
And shed fresh lustre on the vivid story,
Which glow'd in sculpture, of his deeds of glory.
What storms could gather in these cloudless skies?
Who dared to call themselves his enemies?

He would have spoken ; but again he hears
  That death-knell in his ears—
 " Ere forty suns have risen on Nineveh,
  Her guilt and glory shall have ceased to be !"
And Conscience whisper'd, 'Tis Jehovah saith,
Till dread conviction ripen'd into faith.
He rose from off his kingly throne of state ;
He laid aside his purple robe ; he sate
In sackcloth and in ashes : his decree
Sped with wild speed through guilty Nineveh :
And all men trembled, and obey'd the word—
" Let neither man, nor cattle, flock, nor herd,
Or food or water taste by night or day ;
But turn ye from the evil of your way,
And mightily implore the God of heaven,
If it may be our crimes can be forgiven."

  *   *   *   *

 Though the stern struggle of his mission o'er,
 The fainting prophet is himself no more ;
 Though seeing Nineveh is spared, he prays
  To finish here his days :

Scorn not the weakness of his faithless fear,
But bend with him a reverential ear,
And catch those gracious accents from above,
Which fill'd his soul with tenderness and love :—
" Thou hast had pity on thy gourd's delight,
Which came, and grew, and wither'd in a night;
Shall I not pity Nineveh, wherein
 Are numberless and guiltless herds and sheep,
 And infants weeping while their mothers weep,
But knowing nothing of their mothers' sin ?"

 Ah, silence here is eloquent—he heard—
 His heart was touch'd—he answer'd not a word.

XIX.

Thus lower'd the storm of vengeance, drear and dark :
 Its folds of ruin wrapp'd the noon-day sky :
Heaven's thunders murmur'd coming wrath. But
  hark !
 From that great city one repentant cry
 Rose like a fragrant incense-cloud on high.

        G

And mercy pleaded and prevail'd : it pass'd,

    And left her in her scatheless majesty :

  The blue heavens smiled, so lately overcast,

Of her unclouded skies the loveliest and the last.

XX.

Woe to the land of Asshur !—after-years

    Too soon forgat the warning voice of Heaven :

And mock'd derisively their fathers' fears,

    And proudly strove with God as they had striven,

    Unheeding, unrepentant, unforgiven.

Ah, woe for Nineveh—the tempest lay

    From off the skirts of her horizon driven,

But ready to descend with baleful sway

The moment God announced her fatal judgment-day.

XXI.

Have ye exhausted all the mines of Ind ?

    Have Egypt's dark-brow'd captives all been sold ?

Or doth the idle unproductive wind

    No more from Tarshish waft her stores untold

    Of spices and of purple and of gold ?

Why grasp ye at the solitary gem,

    Which, from all jewels of the earth, of old

The Lord hath chosen for his diadem—

The favourite land of heaven—beloved Jerusalem?

XXII.

Oh weep with weeping Israel! Broken-hearted,

    Far off she mourns, the Gentile's prisoner:

Her beauty and her bloom hath all departed,

    For her transgressions great and grievous were;

    And therefore hath the Lord afflicted her[7].

Like some wild vision of the night it seems—

    Her old men crave a speedy sepulchre;

Her sons in fetters foster hopeless dreams;

Her daughters hang their harps by far ungenial streams.

XXIII.

Yet half the tempest fell not: Jordan still

    Fenced Carmel's forest and Siloah's spring.

But lo, a darker tempest-cloud of ill!

    Innumerable hosts were marshalling

    Beneath the banners of Assyria's king—

[7] Lamentations i. 5.

Wilt thou not manifest thy glory there ?

   Wilt thou not spread, O Lord, thy guardian wing ?

Wilt thou not listen to that piercing prayer ?

" Spare us, O Lord our God—spare us, Jehovah, spare."

XXIV.

On like a vulture to the field of doom

   Sennacherib came hasting thro' the land ;

He march'd in vengeance, like the fierce Simoom

   With clouds and pillars of hot burning sand,

   That sweeps o'er Afric's desolated strand.

Proudly he taunted Heaven, and ask'd in wrath,

   What God or man his armies could withstand ?

Fool, fool, who never in his blood-stain'd path

Had wrestled with the calm omnipotence of faith.

XXV.

'Twas midnight, when the angel of the Lord

   Went forth and look'd upon that teeming glen,

And waved above that host his silent sword ;

   Nor sheathed the fearful blade of death again

   Till more than eighteen myriads of men

Slept their last slumber on the blasted heath.

   In fear the scanty remnant fled, and when

The morning rose, no living man drew breath

In that vast host of slain—that silent camp of death [8].

XXVI.

But woe to thee, Assyria, who hast striven

   To mock Jehovah with thine impious tongue;

Guard thine own city from the bolts of heaven!

   Thy hour is coming.   Zion's virgin young

   Already hath thy funeral dirges sung:

Already Israel's bard has seized the lyre [9],

   The awful lyre of prophecy, and flung

These scathing words of heaven's avenging ire,

To brand thy withering pride with everlasting fire.

'Tis the Lord—'tis the Lord—'tis the glorious God,

He hath smitten the earth with the curse of His rod,

---

[8] Isa. xxxviii.

[9] Nahum; he appears to have uttered his burden of Nineveh, which the writer has attempted to paraphrase in the following lines, the very year, B.C. 713, in which Sennacherib invaded Judæa.

And the nations stand at His judgment-seat:
The lightnings and thunders His mission perform,
The Lord hath His way in the whirlwind and storm,
   And the clouds are the dust of His feet.
He rebuketh the sea, and a desert is made,
   And the rivers are dust at His word,
And Bashan, and Carmel, and Lebanon fade,
And the earth is consumed, and the hills are dismay'd,
   The depths of the mountains are stirr'd.
Say, who can stand in His anger's path
   When his fury descends like fire?
Say, who can abide the heat of His wrath,
   For the rocks are rent by His ire?

The Lord is good, and a hiding-place
For those who in trouble seek His face;
Behold, on the mountains are those who tell
Of peace and salvation to Israel.

Proud Nineveh! are thy watchers dumb?
The hosts that shall dash thee in pieces are come.
Ho! man the ramparts, watch the way,
And set thy battle's fierce array:

The shields of thy mighty men are red,

And thy valiant men are in scarlet clad;

Like flaming torches thy chariots seem,

And run like the lightning's vivid gleam,

And the cry resounds through those dense alarms,

Stand, Asshur, stand—To arms! To arms!

Huzzab is fallen: void and vast,

All at her death-pangs stand aghast;

And the loins are loosed with pain at her doom,

And the faces of all men gather gloom.

Where is the lions' rifled lair?

The dens of prey and of ravine, where?

Woe to the bloody city, woe!

The Lord hath smitten her, and lo!

Drunken she staggers to and fro.

Who lately sate a Princess seeming,

With witcheries and whoredoms teeming;

And far her proud defiance hurl'd,

The harlot empress of the world;—

How is she dragg'd in chains along!

Why beats she her breast at the victor's song?

How lies she friendless, shelterless,

In guilt, and shame, and nakedness!

The gazing-stock of those who were
Once slaves and sycophants of her!
The sharp fire burns like the cankerworm,
And the sword has defiled thy alluring form;
But never hath a balm been found
To heal thy everlasting wound.
Earth waves exultingly its hand
O'er thee, the scourge of every land.

XXVII.

These harpings ceased, and when I look'd again,
Fire, sword, and famine their fell work had done.
The city lay in ruin on the plain:
Her shrines, her palaces, her monarch's throne,
One mingled mass of crumbling earth and stone.
Time digg'd thy grave, and heap'd the dust on thee;
Soon died the echo of thy dying groan;
And travellers, who came thy wreck to see,
Ask'd, and received no answer—Where is Nineveh?

XXVIII.

. . . It is the evening of the world. The sun
Casts level shadows o'er its restless tide;
And though dense clouds, before his race be run,

Betoken coming tempest, in their pride
  The nations still all signs of night deride,
And to and fro are hurrying thro' the earth
  By ancient tracks or pathways yet untried
To satisfy their souls' insatiate dearth
With riches or with fame, or pleasure's idiot-mirth.

XXIX.

Men throng all paths of knowledge, urging still
  Into the vast unknown their perilous way ;
Wielding all powers of nature to their will,
  To-day they spurn the speed of yesterday,
  And travel with the storms, nor brook delay.
And swifter than the eagle's swiftest wing
  They bind their words upon the lightning's ray,
And from the elements new virtues wring,
To sound the lowest depths of truth's exhaustless spring.

XXX.

Men throng all paths of knowledge. Science dives
  Below the ocean's bed, the mountain's base,
And from the bowels of creation rives
  Those monumental stones which dimly trace

Earth's primal story: then she soars apace
Above our little orb, and speeds afar
    Mid distant planets her unwearied chase,
  Skirting their track as in a seraph's car
From luminous world to world, from gorgeous star to star.

XXXI.

Men throng all paths of knowledge. It might seem
    Earth was now launch'd upon the early source
Of time's illimitably-flowing stream ;
    But trace the windings of her backward course,
    Her centuries of crime and dark remorse,
And learn these struggles ne'er can be renew'd ;—
    The feverish efforts of exhausted force,—
The latest ebb of strength almost subdued,—
The sure and fearful signs of near decrepitude.

XXXII.

See how upon those ancient haunts she dwells,
    Where first her prowess and her power began ;
And lingers there instinctively, and tells
    Her antique story like an aged man,

Telling what races in his youth he ran,

And all the trophies of his early prime; `

Too conscious that his brief remaining span

Waits only for the solemn passing chime,

To warn us he hath done with all the things of time.

XXXIII.

She treads again the wastes of Babylon,

.And roams amid Etrurian tombs once more,

And fondly lingers where the setting sun

Gilds ancient Carthage, or the fabled shore,

Where Greece and Troy were lock'd in fight of yore,

And listens to their story as the last

Faint halo of a day too quickly o'er;

For soon her bright futurity shall cast

Into deep twilight shade the glory of the past.

XXXIV.

And what although this latest age hath riven

The veil which hides thy shames, O Nineveh,

From all the taunts of earth and frowns of heaven;

Though distant nations crave admiringly

Some relic or some monument of thee;
Though from far lands the lonely traveller
    Wanders thy ruin and thy wreck to see ;—
Who shall recall to life the things that were ?
Or wake the spectral forms of thy vast sepulchre ?

XXXV.

No, while the ages of this shatter'd world
    Roll slowly to the final term of time,
There shalt thou lie in desolation, hurl'd
    By vengeance from that pinnacle sublime
    Whereon thou satest in thy glory's prime—
By travellers of every nation trod,
    Jehovah's warning unto every clime,
Scathed with His anger, smitten with His rod,
And witnessing to man the eternal truth of God.

Banningham, 1851.

EZEKIEL.

A SEATONIAN PRIZE POEM.

"O navis, referent in mare te novi
　　Fluctus?　O quid agis? fortiter occupa
Portum."

A DAY of many clouds, and sudden showers,
And breaks of golden sunshine!—calmly now
On yonder cottage of the valley, lying
Embosom'd in the guardian hills and woods,
Rests, like a father's smile, the parting flush
Of evening: and of all the frequent storms
But few have broken on the peasant's roof
In that sequester'd glen; and, having shed
Their quick tears almost ere they woke alarm,
Pass'd as a dream in lucid light away.
But he whose watch is builded on the ridge

Of the snow-crested Apennines, awe-struck
Has mark'd the rising storm-clouds one by one,
The which have cast their shadow on his soul,
Though most have parted to the right or left,
And fall'n on other lands.   Such was thy life,
Ezekiel, prophet of the Lord of Hosts,
And sentinel of Israel's destinies.
Let others nestling in secluded homes,
The narrow circle of themselves and theirs,
Ask of the present hour its joy or grief:—
Thy eagle soul was nursed and nerved to climb
Through winds and tempests sun-ward, or to stand
Alone upon the everlasting hills,
And with a patriot's and a prophet's eye
Read the vex'd future, and the calm beyond.

Dark are the landscapes of a fallen world,
And dark must be the thunder-clouds that roll
Above them; and no eye but His who dwells
Pavilion'd in eternity, and sees
The everlasting Sabbath imaged there,
Might dare to scan in comprehensive view

The desolations of six thousand years[1].

His hand was on thee, holy seer[2]: His voice

Commission'd thee as His ambassador

To Israel and the nations: but or ever

He bared the secrets of futurity,

In mystic vision He unveil'd Himself,

The brightness of His glory, the express

Image of His eternal Godhead[3].   Else,

Ezekiel, had thy soul unequal proved

To grasp the awful counsels of His will,

Or haply had been lifted up, like his

Who, first and noblest of created beings,

Son of the morning, peerless Lucifer,

Fell ruinous from heaven, and with him dragg'd

Bright myriads into outer darkness down.

But never minstrel uninspired may catch

The stern unearthly music of thy harp

[1] "No eye but His might ever bear
    To gaze all down that drear abyss,
  Because none ever saw so clear
    The shore beyond of endless bliss."—*The Christian Year.*
[2] Ezek. i. 3.   [3] Heb. i. 3.

Prophetic, nor with imitative notes

Tell what thou saw'st, where Chebar's crystal waves

Refresh'd thy solitary exile: when

There came dense cloud and whirlwind from the north,

And fiery wreaths of flame, fold within fold, ·

And brightness as of glowing amber, round

Those living creatures inexpressible[4].

Of human likeness seem'd they, clad with wings

Of Cherubim, like burning coals of fire

Or lamps that flash'd as lightnings to and fro;

Straight moving, where the Spirit will'd.   Beneath

Wheels rush'd, set with innumerable eyes,

Wheel within wheel of beryl, and instinct

With one pervading Spirit: over-head

The firmament of crystal, terrible

In its transparent brightness stretch'd.   They rose,

And lo, the rushing of their wings appear'd

The roll of mighty waters, or the shout

Of countless multitudes: until, the voice

Of God above them sounding eminent,

Straightway they stood and droop'd their awful wings.

[4] See Ezek. i. and x.

And far above the firmament behold
The likeness of a sapphire throne : and there,
Mysterious presage of the Incarnate, shone
The likeness of a man ; human He was
In every lineament, yet likest God,
Clad with the glory of amber and of fire :
Pure light amid the impenetrable dark,
Insufferably radiant, till it wrote
The arch of mercy on the clouds of wrath,
And with its zone of soften'd rainbow hues,
Gold, emerald⁵, and vermilion, spann'd the throne.

His hand was on thee, prophet, in that hour:
Prostrate in adoration at His feet
His voice revived thee, or thy soul had sunk
Unstrengthen'd to endure such massive weight
Of glory.   But enough—thine eyes have seen
The King, the Lord of Hosts, Emmanuel ;
And henceforth in the panoply of God
Arm'd, thou canst front the lowering looks of man,
The powers of hell discomfit, and athwart

⁵ " In sight like unto an emerald."—Rev. iv. 3.

II

The troublous ocean-floods of time look forth
Firm as the rooted rocks.   Such hidden springs
Of strength the vision of the Almighty gives.
So he who bow'd before the burning bush
Quail'd not in Pharaoh's presence.   He who led
The hosts of Israel forth victoriously,
First stood before their Captain and his own
And worshipp'd⁶.   But the time would fail to tell
Of Mamre's plain, and Peniel's midnight hour,
Of warriors, and the goodly fellowship
Of prophets, and apostles, who beheld
In vision or in blest society
Jehovah's glory, ere they turn'd to flight
The armies of the aliens, or proclaim'd
His advent, or in faith impregnable
Storm'd the proud ramparts of a rebel world,
And on the crumbling citadel of Rome
Raised gloriously the standard of the Cross.

Nor needless was the strength of heaven: for bleak
And bitter were the wintry storms that swept

⁶ "As Captain of the host of the Lord am I now come."—Josh. v. 14.

Thy destined path, Ezekiel: unto grief
No stranger thou.   Softly thy childhood smiled
Around thee in thy far-off fatherland:
A mother's tears of joy upon thy cheeks
Had fallen, brief as dewdrops, which the Spring
Sips from the waking flowers; and through thy soul
A father's benediction had diffused
Its life-long balm: and soon the priesthood claim'd
In Salem's courts thy white-robed ministries.
How dear the memories of that holy shrine
Amid unrest and exile!   Israel's sins
Had drain'd the last of heaven's long-suffering,
And vengeance might not slumber more.   The storm,
Whose skirts enfolded Palestina, fell
Upon thy guilty walls, Jerusalem,
With fiercest bolts of ruin and of wreck[7].
Before its path the land of Eden bloom'd,
Behind there lay one desolate wilderness.
Nor now avails it from a thousand homes
Blacken'd with blood and flames, to single thine:

[7] Ezekiel apparently began his prophecy about five years after second captivity.

One of the darkest pictures which the Past
Hides trembling.   Fatherless and motherless,
Reft of thy brethren, home, and native land,
Torn from the bleeding altars of thy God,
They spared thee to adorn the purple pride
Of Asshur's triumph, and then cast thee forth
To hang thy exiled harp by Chebar's streams.

Little they dream'd in their delirious mirth
The might that slumber'd in those shatter'd chords.
Thy spirit was bruised, not broken: time has lost
Its spell—eternity has fill'd thy heart:
Thy early home is drench'd with tears and blood,
And, lo, before thee rises dimly grand
Thy mansion in the heavens.   What if the dews
And summer rivulets of life, its fresh
And first affections, have been wither'd up
Untimely, in thy spirit's inmost depths
Unseen the springs of heavenly love gush forth,
And make low music in the ear of God.

His hand was on thee, and His Spirit breathed

In thy stern oracles, what time alone

Thou wentest forth in bitterness of soul,

Unbending, unattracted, undismay'd,

With adamantine forehead to confront

Faces of adamant and hearts of stone[8]:

Seven days a voiceless witness, communing

With God in silence.   But the Sabbath came[9],

And with it all its holy memories,

And thoughts of Zion and Jerusalem;

And, breeze-like from the hills of heaven, again

The echo of angelic harmonies,

And rushing of the wings of cherubim

Swept o'er thy spirit.   Then thy tongue was loosed;

Nor longer mute, the harp of prophecy

Woke to thy raptured touch its strains of fire.

" Woe to the wicked! he shall surely die;

Woe to the iron heart, and right hand clench'd

Against the widow and the fatherless!

[8] Ezek. iii. 8, 9.

[9] " I . . . . remained there astonished seven days . . . . and it came to pass at the end of seven days that the word of the Lord came to me."— Ch. iii. 15, 16. This has been thought to allude to the Sabbath.

Woe to the murderer, the rebellious son,

The daughter revelling in harlotry,

The faithless wife, the dark adulterer,

The sin-polluted homes of Israel !

Woe unto him who leaves the living God,

Insensate, to adore upon the hills

His idol deities of lust and blood!"

Woe to the land that hath abandon'd God;

God hath abandon'd her: His glittering sword

Is whetted, and His winged arrow lies

Upon the string.   The sentence is gone forth.

The messengers of death are on their way,

The sword of noon, the pestilence that walks

In darkness, and the ravening beasts of prey.

Behold the fury of Omnipotence,

The wrath of the Eternal! who shall stand

His vengeance? for the roll of fate is fill'd

With mourning and lament and wrath and woe.

It ceased awhile, that wail of prophecy;

But fraught with darker mysteries ere long

Swell'd, like the moanings of the wintry wind

Again and yet again around the stones
Of crumbling sepulchres.   Thine eyes have seen,
O Lord, the chambers of dark imagery,
The women weeping at the idol shrine
Of Tammuz, and those worshippers who kneel
In vile prostration to the rising sun[1].
Woe for the bloody city! seeing not
Those awful watchers standing at her gates
White-robed, and girt with weapons keen as death[2]:
Nor hearing in her giddy mirth the words
That fell, Ezekiel, on thy anguish'd soul—
" Go through the gates, go through the streets, and slay—
Slay old and young, virgin and suckling child,
Spare not, but slay ye every thing that breathes;
Save those few sealed ones who sigh and cry
In secret bitterly before their God."

Woe for apostate Salem! she forsakes
Her glory, and the glory of the Lord
Forsakes His temple.   Lingering and slow[3]

---

[1] Ezek. viii. 5—18.   [2] Ezek. ix. 1—7.
[3] See Ezek. x. 18; xi. 22, 23.

As loth to leave His chosen heritage,
From court to court the cloud of brightness swept,
And on the threshold brooded, awfully
Reluctant; but anon the cherubim
And wheels, and sapphire throne, and firmament
Of crystal, moving silently, forsook
Thy gates, O Zion: and a little space
Resting upon the brow of Olivet,
When the last sands of mercy had run out,
Rose like a golden sunset-cloud, impress'd
With living light, and as it vanish'd left
A track of glory in the desolate heaven.

Joy once for beautiful Jerusalem!
Hers was the time of love[4], when cast abroad
A helpless infant in her blood, she wept
And soon had wept her last: but lo! the Lord
Pass'd by, and o'er her His wide mantle threw,
And chose her, and embraced her with the arms
Of mercy.　And she grew in loveliness
And love: her breasts like sculptured ivory

[4] Ezek. xvi. 1—14.

Or roes that feed among the lilies[5]: grace
Flow'd in her movements; and her golden hair
About her like a veil transparent waved.
Her raiment was of broider'd needlework,
And silks of richest dyes; and Ophir hung
Her hands with bracelets, and her neck with chains;
And jewels, sparkling as the dew-drops, lit
Her coronet of gold.   But none may tell
Her trancing and unearthly comeliness,
For heaven apparell'd her in robes divine[6],
Hers was the perfect beauty of her God.

Ah, woe for faithless Salem! where is now
The love of her espousals? guilt and grief
Have written on her brow their frequent tale.
It was a picture too unstain'd for earth,
And sin has marr'd a second Paradise,
When she the loveliest, most beloved of brides,
Sank harlot-like in base adulterous arms.

[5] Song iv. 5.

[6] "It was perfect through My comeliness which I had put upon thee."—Ezek. xvi. 14.

The curse has fallen on thee: bitter tears
Of blood and anguish have been wept: thy bloom
Is trampled in the dust, thy charms exposed
To every gazer's ridicule; and none
But God could pardon thee.   But hark! He speaks[7]
Of pardon, and of early covenants
Of free forgiveness, and a happier home
Of silent love and humble trustfulness.

But Israel was not lonely in her guilt,
Nor lonely was her chastisement.   Beside
The flowing waves of Chebar rose the strains
Of prophecy which after years have sung
As dirges of the fall of many lands.
Proud Moab sunk before those prescient words,
More terrible than thunder, or the shout
Of conquering foes: and scoffing Idumæa
Grew pale: and haughty Philistina fell,
And Egypt with her hoary honours sank
Debased[8].   But chiefly she, who on the rocks
Sate moated by the ocean waves, and seem'd

      [7] Ezek. xvi. 60—63.   [8] Ezek. xxv.; xxix. 14.

A God unto the nations, peerless Tyre,
Wither'd beneath the unsuspected notes,
Lone prophet, of thy awful harp.   Long years
In beauty had she walk'd the waters : pride
Had deck'd her prow, and perfected her shape.
Her masts were cedars hewn on Lebanon,
Her oars were oaks of Bashan, and her boards
Of pine : her sails were of Egyptian woof,
Twined blue and purple, and her mariners
From Zidon, Tyrian pilots at the helm.
Her merchants were the nations of the earth,
Tarshish and Tubal and the tents of Cush,
Damascus, Sheba, Araby the blest,
Asshur, and Dan, and Javan.   And her freights
Were treasures bought or won from every-land ;
Horses and mules, silver and gold, and brass,
Ebon and ivory and emeralds,
Coral and agate, finest flour of wheat,
Honey and oil and balm, and luscious wines,
And spices, cassia, nard, and frankincense,
And lambs and snowy fleeces, and the rams
Of Kedar, and embroider'd robes of blue,

And every rich, and every gorgeous thing.

Who might compare with thee, unrivall'd Queen?

Alas, alas! thy rowers in their pride

Have brought thee into perilous waters—vain

Their skill and numbers—for the Eastern blast

Through rent sails and through riven bulwarks sweeps:

And thy rich merchandise, the gather'd wealth

Of ages, cast into the boiling surge

Perfumes the storm with spices, robes the waves

With purple and with scarlet, and with pearls

And gold enriches the insatiate deep.

Nothing can save thee now.   A bitter cry

Of lamentation from thy sinking crew,

Echo'd by wailing ships and weeping shores,

Rises to heaven; and on the billows float

Huge fragments scatter'd by the winds adrift,

Or cast by after tempests on the rocks,

Thy former throne, and now thy sepulchre[9].

And shall the wrathful lightnings that have scathed

All nations, and the chosen land of heaven

[9] See Ezek. xxvi.—xxviii.

Leave thee unhumbled, Asshur? Thou hast grown
As grows the stately cedar fed with dews,
And nourish'd by the snows and rivulets,
Upon the peaks of Lebanon, until
It rises terribly pre-eminent,
And o'er the forest casts its haughty shade.
But soon the storm fell on thee. Vainly now
Thy iron roots are wrapt about the rocks,
For thou art scorch'd and blasted by the bolts
Of heaven, and hewn by many a ruthless arm
Of those who underneath thy branches slept
Ungrateful: now the lair of prowling beasts,
Or resting-place of cruel birds of prey[1].

Cease thy dark harpings, prophet of the Lord,
Cease, for thy voice and stormy visions cast
Their desolations on the soul of him
Who hears entranced, yet cannot choose the while
But listen. Hark! the prophet lays his hand
Once more upon the trembling chords, and lo,
A valley[2], desolate as Tophet, fill'd .

[1] See Ezek. xxxi.   Ezek. xxxvii. 1—14.

With bones innumerable, sere and bleach'd,

As though the sudden pestilence of God

Had fallen on some mighty host, and men

Had left them in the sun and winds to rot.

Death brooded o'er them.   But a voice from heaven

Startles the awful silence: and behold

A shaking, and the bones, bone to his bone,

Together framed the perfect skeleton;

And sinews cover'd them, and flesh and skin,

The very lineaments of life.   Again

The prophet's voice falls on them: and the winds

Breathe like the quickening Spirit of the Lord

Above the lifeless slain: and lo, they rose

An army numberless, equipp'd for fight.

Hope rises from despair, and life from death.

Ha! the dense clouds are breaking: mighty winds

Have rent a pathway through their gloom, and far

Across the everlasting mountains gleam

The faint streaks of the morning.   What if soon

One more prophetic vision scatters woe

On Meshech and the prince of Tubal's host[3],

<hr>

[3] Ezek. xxxviii. xxxix.

The last stupendous sacrifice of war
Reeking to heaven from Armageddon's vale:—
It passes like a haggard dream away,
And in the far horizon (joy for thee,
Ezekiel, lonely watchman of the night)
Grow clearer and more clear the roseate hues
Of morning-land: and here and there peep forth
The stars in dewy paleness, soon to fade
Before the glory of the rising Sun,
Rising with healing in His wings. He comes,
And in the mellow light which ushers in
His advent, to thy searching ken, O seer,
Stand forth the turrets of His temple[4], built
Of goodlier stones, and bright with fairer light
Than Solomon in all his glory saw:
With holy courts, and incense clouds of praise,
And deep memorial rites. He comes, He comes,
With rushing wings, and calm crystalline throne:
The same who came to thee by Chebar's banks
And lighten'd thy lone exile: now the earth
Shines with the beauty of His countenance,
And heaven rings forth its welcome jubilee.

[4] Ezek. xl.

The hills have caught the tidings from the sky,

Which o'er them bends in brightness; and the glens

Repeat the promise to re-echoing glens;

The ocean with its music, myriad-voiced,

Bears on its heaving breast the rapturous sound

Of Hallelujah, and the morning stars

Sing welcome, and the sons of God again

Shout in their everlasting homes for joy.

Enough for thee, Ezekiel, to have caught

The echo of that music: when the harp

Of all creation, jarr'd too long by sin

And grating discords manifold, at last

Retuned and temper'd by the hand of God,

Shall yield to every breath of heaven, that sweeps

Across its countless and melodious strings,

Eternal songs of gratitude and love.

Hinton Martell, 1854.

JOHN BAPTIST.

ἀστὴρ πρὶν μὲν ἔλαμπες ἐνὶ ζώοισιν ἑῶος,
νῦν δὲ θανὼν λάμπεις ἕσπερος ἐν φθιμένοις.

Soft the summer sun is sinking through the saffron sky to
rest:

Soft the veil of sultry vapour trembles on the desert's
breast;

Golden, crimson, purple, opal lights and shadows, warp and
woof,

Wrap the sands in change, and flush Machærus' battlemented
roof.

Saying, "'Tis my last," a captive rose from the cold dungeon
floor,

Clank'd the fetters with his rising, lean'd the grated lattice
o'er,—

Gaunt albeit in manhood's prime, as he through bitter toils
    had pass'd,

" One look more on earthly sunsets ; my heart tells me, 'tis
    the last."

In his eye the fading sunlight linger'd on as loth to go,

Light to light akin and kindling, brother-like ; and to and
    fro,

As the winds crept o'er the desert from the hills of Abarim,

From his brow his unshorn tresses flutter'd in the twilight
    dim.

Now and then a passing glory from the castle's banquet hall,

Where a thousand lamps bade thousand guests to royal
    festival,

Smote the topmost turret's ridges with a gleam of fitful
    light,

As the woven purple hangings, sail-like, caught the gales of
    night :

Now and then a gush of laughter ; now and then a snatch
    of song,

Seem'd to mock the prisoner's vigil, and to do his silence
    wrong.

Never a word spake he; but, gazing on the hills and skies
    and stars,
Free in thought, as Arab ranger, maugre manacles and
    bars,
Lived again his life, its daybreak with no childish pastimes
    boon,
Morning, midday, and now evening, ere it well was afternoon.

Meet his early homestead: westward of that sea where
    plies no skiff,
On the bare bleak upland, nestling only to the rugged cliff,
Far from all the noise of cities, far from all their idle mirth,
Where God's voice was heard in whispers, and the heavens
    were near to earth,
There he grew, as grows the lonely pine upon the foreland's
    crest,
Fronting tempests, northward, southward, sweep they east
    or sweep they west,
Wrapping round the rocks her roots like iron bands in
    breadth and length,
Here and there a moss or lichen shedding tenderness on
    strength.

Thus he grew : the child of age, no brother clasp'd in equal
    arms,

No sweet sister throwing o'er him the pure magic of her
    charms;

Heir of all his father's ripe experience both of things and
    men,

Ripen'd by the mellow suns that shine on threescore years
    and ten ;

Heir of all his saintly mother's burning concentrated love,

Pent for decades and now loosen'd by a mandate from above.

For the rest, no human friendship shared his fellowship
    with God,

Lonely like the lonely Enoch was the path his spirit trod:

Meet for him whose fearless banner was ere long aloft
    unfurl'd,

God's ambassador, Christ's herald, in a lapsed and guilty
    world.

Gliding years pass'd on ; and childhood grew to youth,
    and youth to prime:

Bodings fill'd the land, and rulers call'd the age a troublous
    time.

Let it be—all time is troublous; and there is no crystal
    sea

Betwixt Eden and the trumpet ushering in the great
    To be.

Nathless storms were rife, and rumours each the other
    chased from Rome,

Though their echo knock'd but feebly at the porch of that
    far home;

And they scarcely stirr'd the pulses in the old man's languid
    heart,

As he pled the prayer of Simeon, " Let me now in peace
    depart;"

Scarcely jarr'd the heavenly foretastes of the rapt Elizabeth,

Oft as was her wont repeating, " Welcome life, thrice
    welcome death."

Droop'd they both with drooping autumn, with the dying
    year they died,

And in one deep stony chamber slumber sweetly side by
    side ;

But before they slept confided to the Baptist's ear a story,

Richer heir-loom, loftier honour than the wide world's
    wealth and glory :—

From his sire he heard the marvel of his own predestined
  birth,
From his mother's lips a mystery which transcends all
  things of earth.

Now the lonely home was lonelier, now the silence more
  unmarr'd,
Now his rough-spun dress was rougher, and his hardy fare
  more hard.
Yet he moved not. God who guided Israel o'er the trackless waste,
When his hour was come, would call him; and with God
  there is no haste.
Meanwhile of all sacred stories, which his bosom fired and
  fill'd,
One, the Tishbite, more intensely through and through his
  bosom thrill'd.
O that sacrifice on Carmel;—O that fire that fell from
  heaven;—
O that nation's shout "Jehovah;"—O that bloody stormy
  even;—

O that solitary cavern;—O that strong and dreadful wind;

Rocking earthquake, flames of vengeance; O that still small
Voice behind:

Those long years of patient witness, crown'd by victory at
last:

Israel's chariot, Israel's horsemen! like a dream the vision
pass'd.

"Would to God the prophet's mantle might but fall upon
my soul!

Would to God a seraph touch me with Esaias' living coal!"

As he pray'd, his soul was troubled with a sudden storm of
thought,

And again was hush'd in silence with profounder feeling
fraught:

And the Spirit's accents,—whether on his mortal ear they fell,

Or without such audience trembled on his spirit, none might
tell,

But they came to him. The altar had been built and piled
and laid:

God himself alone must kindle that which He alone had
made.

Through the crowded streets of Salem, see, they whisper
    man to man,

Like a flash of summer lightning through the heavens, the
    tidings ran ;

" In the wilderness by Jordan unto us a Voice is sent,

God is on His way. His herald cries before He comes,
    Repent."

On the mart of busy traffic, on the merchant's growing hoard,

On the bridegroom's perfumed chamber, on the banquet's
    festive board,

On the halls where pleasure squander'd all the heaps of
    avarice,

On the dreams of blind devotion, on the loathsome haunts
    of vice,

Like a thunder-roll the tidings fell, and lo ! the sudden
    gloom

Then and there gave fearful presage of the coming day of
    doom.

But the workman left his workshop, and the merchant left
    his wares,

And the miser left his coffers, and the Pharisee his prayers :

From Jerusalem to Jordan, see they pour a motley group,

Young men, maidens, old men, children, priests and people,
  troop on troop:

Neighbour thought not now of neighbour, parent scarcely
  thought of child:

There were few who spoke or answer'd, there were none
  who jeer'd or smiled:

No one wept: tyrannic conscience seal'd their eyes and ears
  and lips,

And Eternity was shadowing Time with terrible eclipse.

There it wound that ancient river: there he stood, that
  lonely man.

Is it yet too late? to rearmost some shrank back, some for-
  ward ran: .

Brave men quail'd, and timid women bolder seem'd beneath
  his eye:

Age grew flush'd, and youth grew paler, and the voice was
  heard to cry,

"God is on His way. The Judge already stands before the gate.

Make the lofty low before Him, rugged smooth, and crooked
  straight."

As the multitudes in thousands round him throng'd, a
    timorous flock,

Fell his words like hail in harvest, like the hammer on the
    rock,

Breaking stony hearts to shivers, cloaking, sparing, soften-
    ing nought,

But with lightning flash revealing midnight mysteries of
    thought.

God was Master, man was servant; right was right, and
    wrong was wrong:

Sinners might dream on a little, but the respite was not long.

Good or evil fruit-trees—whether of the twain? no test
    but fruit:

Cut it down; the fire is kindled, and the axe lies at the root.

Wherefore call themselves the children of the God-like
    Abraham?

THINGS THAT ARE alone are precious unto the supreme
    I AM.

Generation bred of vipers, wherefore are they pale and
    dumb?

Will they flee? oh, who hath warn'd them of the dreadful
    wrath to come?

Are the dry bones stirring, breathing? God can raise up
    men from stones.

See the Lamb, the dying Victim! only life for life atones:

And the deep red current, flowing from the firstlings Abel
    vow'd,

Cries from age to age for mercy, louder yet, and yet more loud,

Till the sacrifice be offer'd for the world's stupendous guilt,

And the Lamb of God is smitten on the altar God has built.

Is the hard heart bruised and contrite? Do they weep and
    vow and pray?

It is well; let Jordan's waters wash their loathèd stains away.

But the coming One, whose coming now was every moment
    nigher,

He, the Son of God, baptizes with the Holy Ghost and fire:

In His hand the fan that winnows; at His feet the harvest
    floor;

Chaff the food for quenchless burnings; garner'd wheat for
    evermore.

So it was from dawn to sunset, so it was from day to day,

Thousands coming, thousands going, till the summer wore
    away:

Ever seem'd the voice more solemn, and the message more
    sublime:

Jordan's lonesome fords were crowded like God's hill at
    Paschal time.

When one eve,—the roseate West was watching for the
    tardy sun,—

Mingling with that throng of sinners came the Only Sinless
    One;

And the Master knelt a suppliant, and abash'd the servan
    stood,

While the holy Christ demanded baptism in that cleansing
    flood.

It is done: Messiah rises from the parted waves; and lo,

The blue heavens are rent asunder, and a Dove, more white
    than snow,

From the gates of light descending like a crown of glory
    glow'd,

Moving towards Him, hovering o'er Him, brooding on His
    head, abode:

And a Voice more deep than thunder from the everlasting
    Throne,

"Thou, my Son, my well Beloved, Thou art my delight alone.

This the Baptist heard.   And straightway Love Divine
    his soul possess'd.

Henceforth all his yearning spirit found its centre, knew
    its rest.

Solitudes no more were lonely, wildernesses were not wild:

He had seen the Word Incarnate, seen the Father's Holy
    Child.

And the pure ideal imaged in his heart of hearts was such

That no earthly joys could dim it, and no human sorrows
    touch.

Let the vex'd waves surge around him! Welcome, weariness
    and strife!

Christ was now his peace, his passion—the one passion of
    his life.

He must decrease, Christ must increase, and His kingdom
    know no end.

He had heard the Bridegroom's accents, he was call'd the
    Bridegroom's friend.

Be it that his days were number'd; this was joy enough for
    him;

And his cup of life was mantling to the overflowing
    brim.

Let his lamp grow pale and paler; only let the Sun be bright,
And the day-star hide its radiance in that perfect Light of
    Light.

So his breast grew calm and calmer, less of self and
    selfish leaven;
So the fire burn'd pure and purer, less of earth and more
    of heaven;
And a loftier hope sustain'd him, as his destined path he trod,
Preaching a world-wide salvation, heralding the Lamb of God !
And the voice rang in the palace, as in hovel and in tent,
"Lo the coming One is come: His kingdom is at hand:
    repent."

Herod heard him, and Herodias, seated on their ivory
    throne.
Something in them craved an audience, and he spake to
    them alone;
Spake of sin and death and judgment, things done wrong
    and undone things.
What to him a royal sinner? He had seen the King of
    kings !

Herod trembled: deeds of rapine cluster'd round his bygone
      path,

Spectres of departed passions, harbingers of coming wrath.

Bid them all avaunt for ever! Blot them from his feverish
      view!

Still forgotten crimes are rising, and his tortured soul
      pursue.

He will doff his purple robes, in sackcloth and in ashes
      lie.

What is time? A day dream. Oh, that burning word, eternity!

Not enough? Why looks the Baptist with that fix'd and
      solemn gaze?

Gold and silver, pearls and rubies, on the temple gate shall
      blaze.

Not enough? Why looks the Baptist piercing through his
      soul and life?

Ha! the queen, his royal consort! nay, his brother Philip's
      wife.

Herod shrank, but smiled Herodias, though the gathering
      vengeance drain'd

Lip of blood, and cheek of blushes. Further answer she
      disdain'd,

But arose, drew forth the monarch, said their royal tryst
    was o'er;

And that night in chains the Baptist press'd Machærus'
    dungeon floor.

Thrice since then had spring and summer carpeted the
    earth with flowers;

But those dreary walls unchanging fenced his slow and
    changeless hours,

Save there grew 'twixt blocks of granite from some chance-
    sown seed a fern;

And the captive watch'd it ever with the daylight's first
    return,

Drinking in the earliest sunbeam, beaded with its dewy tears,

All its tender leaflets laden and emboss'd for future years.

And it spake to him. It chanced there visited his lonely
    cell,

Chuza, seneschal of Herod; and a word of power that fell

From the Baptist's lips found lodgment in the deep repose
    of thought

Hidden in a kindred nature, truthful, generous, nobly
    wrought.

So it was, an unknown friendship unsuspected entrance gains

For a love that loved their master better, dearer for his
chains;

Whence he knew ONE name was wafted now on every
passing breath,

Filling Judea's hills and valleys with the fame of Nazareth.

Joy for thee! no weak reed shaken by the fickle fitful
wind:

No soft courtier clothed in raiment woven in the looms of
Ind:

O true prophet, more than prophet! voice of God! Messiah's
friend!

Burning, shining, let thy beacon blaze unwavering to the end!

     *   *   *   *   *

Musing thus his past, the captive on his watch nor slept
nor stirr'd,

And the hours slid by unheeded, and the cock crew twice
unheard:

And the dewy stars more faintly glimmer'd in the doubtful
gloom,

And the bursts of mirth were fewer from the royal banquet
room.

K

Thither Galilee had summon'd all her loveliness and state,

And her loveliest there seem'd lovelier, and her greatness
there more great:

Flow'd the purple wine like water: Eden's perfumes fill'd
the hall;

And the lamps through roseate colours shed a soften'd light
on all.

Mirth and music hand in hand were floating through the
fairy scene;

All were praising Herod's glory, all were lauding Herod's
queen;

When at given sign was silence, and the guests reclined
around,

And a lonely harper, waking from the chords a dreamlike
sound,

Breathed delight and soft enchantment over ear and heart
and soul:

None could choose but list, and listening, none their tenderest thoughts control:

When the young, the fair Salome, from her chamber gently slid,

Nor loose veil, nor golden tresses half her mantling blushes
hid:

Young Salome, sixteen summers scarcely on her bloom had
    smiled;

Art was none, but artless beauty; Nature's simplest fondest
    child.

At the banquet's edge she linger'd, to her mother's side she
    press'd,

And assay'd to dance, and falter'd trembling; but again
    caress'd,

As those wild notes with a stronger witchery on her spirit
    fell,

Stole into the midst, and startled, timid as a young
    gazelle,

Trod the air with printless footsteps, as the breezes tread
    the sea,

Moved to every tone responsive, like embodied melody:

Till embolden'd, as she floated like a cloud of light
    along,

Mingled with melodious music gentler cadences of song,

And when every ear was ravish'd, every heart subdued with
    love,

Dropp'd at length, as drops the skylark from its azure
    home above,

Swiftly with an angel's swiftness, with a mortal's sweetness
sweet,

Glowing, trembling, trusting, loving—dropp'd at length at
Herod's feet.

Heaven be witness, Herod grants her the petition she
prefers:

Half his kingdom were mean dowry for a loveliness like
hers.

To Herodias young Salome fondly turns, with grateful
smiles:

Gold of Ophir, pearls of ocean, nard and spice of happier
isles,—

What of choice and costly treasures, choicest, costliest, shall
she claim?

Then a glare of fiendish triumph in that cruel cold eye
came;

And the queen's heart heaved with vengeance; and she
gasp'd with quicken'd breath

Brief words of envenom'd malice, warrant of the prophet's
death.

Why that sudden ashy pallor? why that passionate caress?

Bends the sapling in the tempest : weakness yields to
    wickedness.

   *   *   *   *   *   *

Musing still his past, the captive on his watch nor slept nor
    stirr'd,

And the dawn drew on unheeded, and the cock crew thrice
    unheard.

Of the sentinels of morning, shining over Abarim,

Only one was left, the day-star; and its lamp was growing dim.

Hark! the bolt is drawn, how slowly: see! the dungeon
    door flung wide:

Weapons gleam along the passage : armed men are by his side.

In their looks he read his sentence, and he knew his hour
    was come,

And his proud neck meekly offer'd to the stroke of mar-
    tyrdom:

And, as flash'd the headsman's broadsword, rose the sun on
    Pisgah's height;

And the morning star was hidden in the flood of golden light.

1868.

THE FAVOURITISMS OF HEAVEN.

In the evening we can longest tarry by the twilight shore,

For at even dreams float on for ever and for evermore:

In the evening stars that glimmer one by one from out the
sky

Tell in tones that touch us nearly how in silence time fleets by:

And a voice like none beside them have the winds of falling
night,

Hurrying on our spirits with them up to Memory's cloudy
height.

In the evening, too, ariseth Hope with all her faëry train,

Turning from the roseate Past to tell us such shall come
again.

And at chiming of the vespers, as it chanced, my thoughts
I cast,

Half awake and half in dreamings, over my far-crowded
Past.

And is 't mine then ?—Some one answers, "How or what is
    it to thee?

Nothing but a train of memories like a silver mist at
    sea :

Here and there a glory scatter'd from the starlight or the
    moon,

Rising like all things of time,—enthusiast! vanishing as
    soon.

Thine the present is—go, grasp it ; thine the future may be
    said ;

But the Past is nothing, nothing but the shadow of a
    shade."

Ceased the voice, and much I wonder'd, but I scarcely dared
    to doubt.

When another spirit answer'd from the silence speaking
    out,—

"Brother, nay—the Past seems vanish'd save to Memory's
    listless eye :

No—no—no—the Past is deathless and its record is on
    high."

List! it rose a heaving landscape, scarce defined yet wondrous strange,

Gloom and glory like a moon-trance flitting o'er in ceaseless change.

There were springs of crystal rapture, rivulets of sorrow too,

Passion with her storm-tost surges, Peace a lake of softest
  blue.

Long my musings like a wanderer wandering o'er the haunts
  of youth,

Slow retraced each bygone feeling in their lucid depths of
  truth,

Till upon love's fount they centred, purest of all waves that
  flow,

Fed itself of heaven, yet feeding all the myriad flowers
  below.

Lean thy heart on mine, beloved,— listen—I have heard
  men say

That the fondnesses of earth will pass with earthly things
  away ;

All the silent eloquence of clasped hands and falling tears,

All the musical low whispers like the music of the spheres,

All the thrilling strange entrancement fluttering over cheek
    and eye,
Like the purple lightning playing with the stars in yon blue
    sky ;—
Things we love, because they tell us of the loving heart
    within,
Feelings of the inmost fountain far beyond the touch of
    sin ;—
These, they say, are human frailties, frailties born of sense
    and time,
But will be no more remember'd when we reach our native
    clime.
There, they say, we all are one, and none can love thee least
    or best,
But as brethren all are equal thro' the myriads of the blest.

It may be an idle question—be my wayward heart forgiven—
How earth's love shall wear the gorgeous bright apparelling
    of heaven.
It may be we are too venturous, for the light is faint and
    dim,
And but little knows the pilgrim of the life of seraphim.

Yet I love to think, mine own one, I shall love thee there
    as here,

Best of all created beings, best of all that angel sphere.

Read we not of earth the seed-time for the glorious world to
    come ?

Faith receiving there her guerdon, sin her saddest dreariest
    doom ?

Have not all the things of life-time issues infinite above ?

And shall love reap there no harvest of the scatter'd seeds
    of love ?

What if now we steep affection oft in weeping, oft in sighs,—

They who sow in tears, beloved, reap the rapture of the
    skies.

True that we can tell but little how the full flood-tide of
    love

Swells from out a thousand rivulets in a thousand hearts
    above ;

True we know not now the rapture, nor a thousandth thou-
    sandth part,

Seeing Him we loved unseen, and face to face and heart to
    heart,

ot a cloud to dim that sunshine, there no sorrow, no alarms,

ut around thee and beneath thee spread the Everlasting
  arms.

here untravell'd worlds of beauty slow unfolding on our
  sight,

pann'd by heaven's eternal rainbow, interwoven love and
  light.

ut those glories none may utter : how should I then tell it
  thee ?

or how faint and far the glimmerings of the waves of
  heaven's Light-sea !

et, mine own one, tell me truly, think'st thou we shall love
  the less ?

'ill that ocean whelm the fountains of thine own true-
  heartedness ?

ark, thy beating heart makes answer in its old familiar
  tone,

All thine own on earth, beloved, and in glory all thine
  own."

Watton, 1844.

TO MY SISTER, ON THE EVE OF HER MARRIAGE.

I.

Thou art leaving the home of thy childhood,
    Sweet sister mine:
Is the song of the bird of the wild wood
    Faint and far as thine?
Listless stray thy fingers through the chords,
Thy voice falters in the old familiar words;
  What wilt thou for the young glad voices
  Wherewith our earliest home rejoices?
    A father's smile benign,
    A mother's love divine,
      Sweet sister mine?

II.

Lay thy hand upon thy mouth, brother,
 Lay thy hand upon thy mouth ;
One word thou hast spoken,—but another
 Were perhaps too much for truth.
Home is left—oh ! yes, if leaving
 Be when home is in our heart :
Grieving—yes, 'tis grief, if grieving
 Be for those who cannot part.
We are one, brother, we are one,—
Since first the golden cord was spun :
It may lengthen, but it cannot sever,
For, brother, it was twined—and twined for ever.

III.

Sister, touch again thy passionate lute—
 Chide no more—chide no more :
Sooner far my voice were ever mute,
 Than to whisper our fond love were o'er.
  But I grieve for hours gone by,
  Of heart to heart, and eye to eye ;
  Oh, we cannot have the joy of meeting
  Day by day thy sunny, smiling greeting;

Nor canst thou a brother's fond caress,

Or a sister's searching tenderness;

Grieve I too for summer flowers,

In calm weather[1]

Cull'd together,

And the merriment of fireside hours.

Something whispers, though our heartstrings cannot sever,

These are gone, sister,—gone for ever.

And for these I must repine,—

Sweet sister mine.

IV.

And my tears shall flow with thine, brother,

At the sound of those quick chimes;

And the thought of home—my father and my mother—

Overfloods my heart at times;

And my grief will have its way:

And though to-morrow

Joy chaseth sorrow,

Sorrow chaseth joy to-day.

[1] "In a season of calm weather"—WORDSWORTH.

Tell me, wherefore should I lull myself asleep ?

Let me weep, brother,—let me weep.

v.

Nay, I will not, cannot, sister, see them flow:

    Weep no more, weep no more.

There is solace from the deepest of our woe,

    That our partings will ere long be o'er.

We are one in joys undying,

    In the family of Heaven,

And we mourn not, like the Pleiads ever sighing,

    " We have lost our sister—we were seven."

Still, however wide our pilgrim footsteps roam,

        Bright and glorious

        Lie before us

Mansions in an everlasting home.

Trust me, sister ; wherefore dost thou weep so sore?

Weep no more, sister,—weep no more.

For my spirit catches all the bloom of thine,

Nor can I in thy prime of bliss repine,

      Sweet sister mine.

DER AUSRUF.

TRANSLATED FROM KÖRNER.

I.

Horror-boding, wild and ruddy,
 Looms the morning, strange as night,
And the sunbeams, cold and bloody,
 Track our bloody path with light:
In the coming hour's bosom
 Clasp'd the fates of nations lie,
And the lot already trembles,
 And there falls the iron die!
There's a claim on thee, brother, of holiest power,
And a pledge to redeem in this dawning hour;
 True in life, true in death, when life has pass'd by.

II.

In the gloom of night behind us
  Lie the haunts our foemen spoke,
And the wrecks that still remind us
  Strangers cleft Germania's oak :
Spurn'd is the tongue we lisp'd in childhood,
  Ruin'd lie our shrines and low,
But our faith is pledged, brethren,
  Haste—redeem that pledge of woe.
There are flames in our land,—up, brethren! and slay,
That the vengeance of Heaven may turn away—
  The Palladium lost redeem from the foe.

III.

Blissful visions lie before us,—
  Lie the future's golden years,—
Stretch blue heavens their curtains o'er us,
  Freedom smiles amid her tears ;
German art and German music,
  Beauty, love's entrancing chain,—
All that's noble, all that's lovely,
  Float in prospect back again.

L

But a death-bearing venture is yet to be pass'd,
On the chance must our life and our life-blood be cast,
And Joy only blooms o'er the victim slain.

IV.

Death—now with our God we'll dare it,
Hand in hand our fate defy,
And our frail heart, sternly bear it
To the altar, there to die.
Fatherland ! at thy great bidding
Here we yield our life for thee,
That our loved ones may inherit
What our blood bequeaths them free.
May thy free oaks, my fatherland, proudly wave
O'er thy children's corse and their silent grave,
And hear thou the oath, and the covenant see.

V.

Give ye yet one blessed token
Of a glance towards beauty's bowers,
Though the poisonous South hath broken
All the bliss of spring-tide flowers ;

Let your eyes be dim with teardrops,
    Teardrops cannot bring you shame ;
Throw ye one last kiss towards them,
    Then to God breathe low their name.
The lips that pray for us at night and at morn,
The hearts that have loved us, the hearts we have torn,
    For them, O our Father, Thy solace we claim.

VI.

On ! now to the battle gory !
    Eye and heart towards yonder light !
Earth is done with, and heaven's glory
    Rises dimly, grandly bright.
Cheer ye, German brethren ! cheer ye,—
    Every nerve in conflict swell ;
True hearts shall be reunited,
    Only for this world farewell.
Hark ! the thunders are rolling, the battle is warm,—
On, brethren, on to the lightning storm !
    Till we meet in a happier world, farewell.

Watton, 1845.

WIEGENLIED.

TRANSLATED FROM KÖRNER.

Oh, slumber softly—on thy mother sleeping
    Thou feelest not life's anguish and unrest;
Thy light dreams know not grief, and fear not weeping,
    And thy whole world is now thy mother's breast.

For, ah! how sweetly' in early hours one dreameth
    When in a mother's love life's dews distil,
Though the dim memory unabiding seemeth
    But a far hope that trembles through me still.

Thrice may this glow pass o'er us sweetly shining;
    Thrice to the happy spirit is it given,
Awhile in Love's celestial arms reclining,
    On earth to picture life's ideal heaven.

For it is she who first the nursling blesses,

    When in bright joys he takes his infant part,

All to his young glance seem to shower caresses,

    Love holds him to his mother's beating heart.

And when the clear blue heavens are clouded over,

    And now his pathway lies through strange alarms,

When first his soul is trembling as a lover,

    A second time Love clasps him in her arms.

Ah, still in storms the floweret's stem is broken,

    And breaks the fluttering heart by tempests riven;

Then Love ariseth with her choicest token,

    And as Death's angel bears him home to heaven.

Watton, 1845.

IN IMITATION OF KÖRNER'S
"DAS WARST DU."

I.

For long o'er life's calm waves I wended,
  Beloved, far from thee alone ;
And many stars my path attended,
And each their tale of music ended
  With warblings of their own.

II.

Strange were the dreams that round me floated,
  And beautiful their various tone,
But like a child on each I doted,
To each my frail heart seem'd devoted,
  For all were then mine own.

III.

And, like a young unpractised singer,
   Who hath nor tears nor sorrow known,
Stray'd through the strings my heedless finger,
If only passing dreams would linger,
   A moment for mine own.

IV.

Then, as a nymph of fabling story,
   Or spirit seen in dreams alone,
Thou passedst by me—a far glory,
Glancing through dim clouds transitory,
   In beauty all thine own.

V.

An hour, and all was still around me:
   But, oh! that vision's magic zone,
It left me not as erst it found me,
But like a strange wild witchery bound me,
   A witchery of its own.

VI.

At last I went, my sail unfurling,
  On life's first billowy waves alone,
Light breezes were the waters curling,
And sunlight every drop empearling,
  With radiance like its own.

VII.

Oh, still that form my spirit haunted,
  Though its deep semblance scarce was known,
Thy steps were on the light clouds planted,
And what of sweetness music chanted
  Seem'd borrow'd from thine own.

VIII.

Beloved, that was blest, but sadness
  Broods alway o'er the heart's unknown:
Now dreams have pass'd, and springs of gladness,
But I may not tell—to tell were madness—
  What joy-springs are mine own.

IX.

Ah! life's rough billows swell for ever,
   And years will fly as years have flown,
And youth fleets on,—yet never, never,
Can time or distance thee dissever,
   Beloved, from thine own.

X.

And still thy form in light arises,
   Like trancing music round me thrown,
And though the voice thyself surprises,
Thy fond love breaks through all disguises,
   And whispers, "All thine own."

Watton, 1844.

ON SEEING A LEAF FALL BY MOONLIGHT.

I.

Oh, bright was the hour when thou wast born,
And the winds sang peace to the blushing morn,
   Who stepp'd o'er the clouds at their matin call:
But ne'er may the memory of days gone by
Save the victim of death when his hour is nigh;
And vain was the warmth of thy natal sky;
     The moonlight saw thee fall.

II.

Thy youth it was spent in dance and glee,
With thy leaflet brothers embowering thee,
   Happiness trembling o'er one and all:

But the loveliest dreams must fade away,

And our comrades, ah, tell me, where are they?

Links are broken to-morrow, though twined to-day;

    The moonlight saw thee fall.

III.

Thou hast stood the cloud and the dashing rain,

Over thee the chill blast hath swept in vain,

  And the night vainly spread her funeral pall:

But a word may crush when the heart doth ache,

And it needs not then a storm ere it break;

Thou hast stood the tempest, when strong hearts quake,

    But the moonlight saw thee fall.

Watton, 1844.

FRAGMENTS.

For though the skirts of the far tempest oft
Have fallen on my path, though I have proved,
At times, the bitterness of grief,—yet, when
The heart is all alone in suffering,
We scarce can say that we have suffer'd ;—all
Seems centred so within us, and the waves
Swell in so narrow and so small a world,
That what hath moved us scarce can ask the name
Of suffering.

———◆———

Sunny hath been my home of childhood—strong
The links of love that bind our happy circle,—
No jarring note hath broken the sweet stream
Of music that hath linger'd, like the dove
Of peace, among us :—father, mother, children—
"Hearts of each other sure," souls knit as one—

All wending in glad fellowship towards Heaven.

Heaven is our bourne, and its far hope hath lighted

Upon our ocean-pathway, beacon-like,

And caught the summits of the smallest waves

That rise and sink around us, telling still

Each bears us onward on its tremulous breast

To the still haven of eternal love.

Sometimes the distant clouds have threaten'd woe,

Their shadow fallen near us, but when we

Were striving to win over our sad hearts,

Unmurmuring to resign what Heaven hath given,

Perchance some floweret from our wreath of love,

Some emerald dew-drop from a cup o'erflowing,—

Then hath our God, our Father, with a smile

That told how He rejoiced in all our joy,

Return'd it to us lovelier, more beloved,

Because for one sad voiceless moment, fear

Had chill'd our hearts lest it should fade or fall.

Watton, 1844.

LINES ON A SUFFERING SISTER.

I.

"IF NEEDS BE."

I.

SUFFERING for thee, sweet sister—and sharp pain—
   For thee, the gentlest of earth's gentle ones ?
Does the cloud gather o'er thy heart and brain
   So darkly, and yet no repining tones ?
Oh, hush ! my own sad heart, thy faithless fears,
And quell or dry thy quick, rebellious tears.

II.

She, as a babe upon a mother's breast,
   A child within a father's sheltering arms,
Unconsciously is lying ;—the unrest,
   Brother, is thine—thine all those rude alarms.
Still thy heart's beatings where she hers hath still'd,
Believing all is best that He hath will'd.

III.

Yet was our home so bright, so passing fair,

    Some faint, dim semblance of a home above ;

And she the tenderest loveliest angel there,

    Around whom cluster'd all our dreams of love :

We thought that grief might never shadow long

What seem'd the fittest haunt for praise and song.

IV.

And was it but a dream ? and has the cloud

    Once and again pass'd by us, threatening woe

And shedding tears ? and has its darkness bow'd

    Our hearts once more in struggling sorrow low ?

And has the sunshine of affection's mirth

Pass'd ever, sleep-like, from this beautiful earth ?

V.

Nay, check your tears, sad sisters, pause and linger,

    And check, sad brother, thy wild wayward words ;

Grief takes thy lyret from thee, and her finger

    Sweeps somewhat rudely o'er the trembling chords.

Ye must not, when beneath the cloud, forget

That He, whose love is sunshine, loves ye yet.

VI.

Methinks I hear His voice of pity saying,—

"Ye clung too closely to your lovely home ;

Your sister's spirit, dear children, is delaying,

To teach ye of a better rest to come :

Where grief is not nor sighing, pain nor tears,

But life, light, love, for everlasting years."

Watton, 1846.

—◆—

II.

"HE GIVETH HIS BELOVED SLEEP."

I.

OH, tread lightly—she is weary,

She hath suffer'd all day through,

And the night is somewhat dreary

If she wake and suffer too:

Silently the stars are keeping

Their sweet vigils o'er her,

And she dreams not in her sleeping

That to-morrow is before her.

II.

Break it not, that spell of slumber,
    Waveless, beautiful as heaven,
'Mid the sharp gusts without number,
    And the clouds, of tempests driven.
Weep not, sister; sister, cheer thee;
    Yet she will not hear thee weep:
She is weary, very weary,
    Only let her sleep.

III.

I could fancy, gazing on her,
    She had pass'd her night of sighs;
And that heaven's own light upon her,
    Waits to greet her opening eyes.
Silence on each word of sorrow,
    On a thought that would repine;
For there shall be such a morrow,
    And for thee, sweet sister mine.

IV.

Ah! I know it, that reposing—
    'Tis her Father bade it come—

M

Emblem, when life's day is closing

Of the deep repose of home ;

Storms the joy of calm redoubling

In the mansions of the blest ;

Where the wicked cease from troubling,

And the weary are at rest.

Watton, 1847.

———◆———

III.

"AND SO HE BRINGETH THEM TO THE HAVEN WHERE
THEY WOULD BE."

YES, billow after billow—see they come

Faster and rougher, as her little boat

Nears evermore the haven.   Oftentimes

It seems to sink and fall adown the wave,

As if borne backward by the struggling tide :

Yet mounting billow after billow, wave

On wave o'er-riding, tempest-tost and shatter'd,

Still, still it nears the haven evermore.

"Poor mariner, art thou not sadly weary?"

Dear brother, rest is sweeter after toil.

"Grows not thine eye confused and dim with sight

"Of nothing but the wintry waters?" True,

But then my pole-star, constant and serene,

Above the changing waters changes not.

"But what if clouds, as often, veil the sky?"

Oh, then, an unseen hand hath ever ta'en

The rudder from my feeble hands the while—

And I cling to it. "Answer me once more,

"Mariner, what think'st thou when the waters bear

"Thy frail boat backward from the long'd-for harbour?"

Oh, brother, though innumerable waves

Still seem to rise betwixt me and my home—

Still billow after billow, wave on wave—

I know that they are number'd: not one less

Should bear me homeward if I had my will;

For One who knows what tempests are to weather,

O'er whom there broke the wildest billows once,

He bids these waters swell. In His good time

The last rough wave shall bear me on its bosom

Into the haven of eternal peace.

No billows after—they *are* number'd, brother.

" Oh, gentle mariner, steer on, steer on :

" My tears shall flow for thee, but they are tears

" In which faith strives with grief, and overcomes."

Watton, 1847.

A NIGHT AT SANDGATE.

IT was a strange and fearful night that same :
We had been talking of the troublous days
That seem'd to lie before us, and the clouds
Of gloom and tempest that were brooding round
The militant church of God : wherein we thought
Not one there gather'd would pass on unscathed.
And yet all hearts beat high, and glistening eyes
Burnt brightly as with coming triumph :—none
Hung back, none trembled, none were sore, afraid.
He, whom unknown we knew, unseen we loved,
Was Pilot of our vessel, and He held
At beck the whirlwinds and the storms and clouds ;
And He seem'd with us, saying ;—"Fear ye not,
Lo! I am with you alway : in the world
Ye shall have tribulation ; let your hearts

Be of good cheer, O ye of little faith,

For I, your Lord, have overcome the world."

So into one another's eyes we look'd,

And found there—sorrow and dismay? nay, found

Such high enthusiast hopes as burn, like stars

'Mid drifting clouds, the brighter at near view

Of sufferings to be suffer'd and for Him,

Of high deeds to be ventured and for Him,

Of peril clasping our affection closer.

Amid that company were two who long

Had held bright standards in the warrior host

Of God—brave hearts—and as we heard them tell

Of conflicts deepening ever on the skirts

Of Christendom's blood-sprinkled battle-field,

The fire and light of love spontaneous rush'd

From heart to heart, and lit their altar-flame.

The evening wore away: and one by one

At length we parted lingering and loth,

For golden are such hours and brief and few:

But drawn, as I divine, by kindred thoughts,

I and one other with me loiter'd yet

By a lone staircase window, that o'erlook'd
The deep blue billows of the midnight sea,
And the swift moonlight on those waters swift;
And overhead the everlasting stars.
But chief three planets look'd into our souls
With their large spirit-eyes. Long while we gazed
In silent rapture on that world of night,
And ponder'd silently, and to the winds
And roar of distant waters listen'd long.
It seem'd a picture of the dread ' to be.'
There were the waters in their ceaseless changes
And wild eternal heavings, white with spray,
Wave chasing wave; but over them the moon
Rode in her silver sphere serene, and chid
Their wildness, and the glancing stars aloft
Fell on them with their sudden tears of light.
A strange and dream-like scene. Yes, soon we spake;
The same thought rush'd upon us—let the world
Change like those changing waters evermore,
And spend itself in moans or reckless smiles,—
Let us be cast upon its fretful waves;
Still stretches o'er us the blue sky, and thence

Lightens the piercing glory of the stars,
The silver beauty of true heart affection.

And like clear village bells at eventide
Each young heart echo'd to the other back,
And ere we parted were there many thoughts
That only could find utterance in prayer.

1845.

ON AN AIR OF NOVELLO'S—AVE VERUM.

COMES it to thee with a sound of joy,
　　Glad-hearted sister mine?
Like the reckless bound of the mountain boy,
　　Or his mirthsome eye divine?

Oh, list again—it has sorrowful deeps,
　　Thou hast not fathom'd yet;
'Tis a loving passionate heart that weeps
　　Tears, none who shed forget.

It speaketh of life,—of beautiful life,
　　A tissue strange and fair,
Yet enwoven with threads of tenderest grief,
　　And dark shades here and there.

It leads the soul to the twilight sky,
   And the stars peep forth in turn,
But a weeping train of clouds is by
   To dim them as they burn.

Speaks it of hope? yes, hope in tears,
   From some far distant shore ;
Music that steals from the nightly spheres,
   Yet sounding, sounds no more.

Watton, 1845.

UNDINE IN MUSIC.

ON THE QUICK MOVEMENT OF MOZART'S SYMPHONY IN E FLAT.

'Twas the twilight dawn at break of day,

And the mists swept over the mountains grey.

Away, away, on thin blue wings,

They flitted across like living things,

      Reckless wanderers they.

Is there a path on those towers of air ?—

'Mid ice and cloud a pathway there ?

Wild are the rocks and interwoven,

But betwixt them a path is dimly cloven.

Ha ! see'st thou aught ?—'tis a waving plume,

And a spear that glances like light through gloom.

'Tis a dashing steed of taintless white :

'Tis a rider's cry—an armed knight.

Now high on the crag ; now deep in the mist,

That at fits the plume of his helmet kiss'd :

As when a light-wing'd bark doth ride
At random o'er the foaming tide :
Now perch'd on the top of the mountain wave,
    Daring the stars for very glee ;
Now hid half-way in the arching cave
    Of the glad exultant sea.
Like to the waves are the wild crags strown,
Like to the bark doth the knight ride on.

Is he in chase of the tumbling rills ?
What seeketh he on the far-off hills ?
There are waves of a rivulet there that stray
    At morning o'er the mountains blue ;
But when the sun rides high, men say,
    It melts like the veriest morning-dew.
Perchance he hath come by that stream to ride :
He reins his steed by a glacier's side.
Was it music ? was it a spell ?
What on the horse and his rider fell ?
For, lo ! by the side of a silver rill
The rider and his horse stood still.

'Tis nought but the sound of gushing waves
Like crystal music in hidden caves,
Tinkling so soft and so clear around,
An angel's whisper, a spirit sound :
Yet it woke the dreams of bygone years,
And won from out his eyes the tears :
For in fitful beauty all unabiding
Were the scenes of his childhood before him gliding.

The spell is broken. He starts away,
The wilder now for the brief delay :
Swift hurries the steed, as one might list,
Yet he lashes him on through storm and mist—
And away ! away ! with might and main,
A playmate of the clouds again.

He curb'd his steed, for he thought he spied
A maiden's robe at his right side.
Is it a maiden beside him lying,
On the far lone mountains in silence dying ?
Ah, no, sir knight—'tis the trembling rill,
That having loved thee, loves thee still,

And follows thee ever through wind and cloud

With whispers loving but not loud.

List! rein thy steed—oh! listen well,

For strange is the music of that soft spell.

" Whither away, dear knight, so fast ?

My tale is not told, my dream is not pass'd :

I melt not away till nigh mid-day :

Gentle knight, whither away ?"

And a shrouded form of silvery mist

Seem'd to float and blend with the waves she kiss'd,

That whether it were a maiden's dress

Or the flow of the streamlet, none might guess.

And the knight stood still.

　　　　　　　　But a stormy sound

Echo'd from forth the caverns round—

'Twas the spirit of the mists who spake.

" No moonlight dreams, Sir Knight, awake !

Away to the reckless chase with me !

I came not in vain from the fetterless sea.

With the blast, as my courser, I'm rushing on
　　　　high

To join in the sport of the stormy sky."

And the knight forgot the lovely stream,
Her music and half-finish'd dream,
And while clatter'd the hoofs like a brazen drum
He shouted afar, "I come ! I come !"

To him the streamlet spake not on:
Her harp strings quiver'd; their tones were gone.
But to the little waves turn'd she,
And thus spake on right cheerily.
" What can tame the spirit proud
Of the knight, who revels in storm and cloud ?
Nothing but tears—and smiles through tears,
And music too sweet for mortal ears.
But I will smile, and I will weep,
And my silver lyre shall wake from sleep.
Flow, sisters, flow in our tuneful stream,
My tale must be told, and finish'd my dream.
Flow merrily, sisters : and track him well.
He hears, he knows, he feels my spell."

The waves flow'd on with their tuneful sound ;
They cross'd the knight in his maddest bound ;

And, like one who sees a spirit-form,

He check'd his course through the cloudy storm:

And bow'd his head, and listens still,

Tranced with the music of the rill.—

And long together side by side

The waves did flow, the knight did ride;

Till the spirit of the streamlet stole

The heart from out his inmost soul.

Oh! stay the hours: the sun rides high:

The tale is told, and the stream must die:

The last few notes, the sweetest far,

Like a trembling voice from a nightly star,

Rich as the tones of a dying swan,

The last few silvery notes are gone.

Watton, 1844.

TEARS IN MUSIC.

ON THE SLOW MOVEMENT OF MOZART'S SYMPHONY IN E FLAT.

I.

Oh, hush! my soul, be silent,
  For the chords sweep on again;
Though it take thy heart from out thee,
  Still listen to the strain.

II.

It flows along, like waters,
  To a tuneful "dying fall,"
And tells of griefs, and tears, and love
  That smiles amid them all.

N

III.

In deep waves of affection
    Flows on the mournful river,
Persuasively, persuasively,
    For ever and for ever.

IV.

Methinks a sad beloved one
    Is by her lover kneeling,
And blent with their own echoes still
    Her tender strains are stealing.

V.

With her soft blue eye she asketh
    The secret of his woe,
For a burning grief hath seal'd his heart
    And his tears will not flow.

VI.

She asketh with the music
    That tells of things that were;
She asks to grieve, for grief with him
    Were a solace unto her.

VII.

Like clouds a bright star circling,
　　Like soft winds round a rose,
Like waters round a lily's brim,
　　That wondrous music flows.

VIII.

Ah, woe for that sweet singer!
　　Woe for that loving heart!
Her pulse beats quick, her words fall fast;
　　But he turns unmoved to part.

IX.

One lingering note recalls him;
　　Thus, thus, he cannot sever:
And on and on persuasively
　　The music flows for ever.

X.

Persuasively, persuasively,
　　She ever seems to plead,
That he would pour his grief to her
　　The saddest, grief could need.

XI.

Her soft blue eye is filling
  With tears for his and him,
And her low sad strain swept on again,
  Until his own were dim.

XII.

Enough, enough—he weepeth,
  His heart no more is cold,
And tears can tell a passionate world
  That in language is untold.

XIII.

Refreshingly as breezes
  Blow o'er the sultry sands,
Refreshingly as gushing showers
  Rain life on thirsty lands;

XIV.

Delicious as when sunshine
  Streams o'er a wintry sky,
Delicious as the soft air's breath
  When the thunder hath pass'd by;

XV.

In trustful calm affection,
    Like some smooth southern river,
Persuasively, resistlessly,
    The music flows for ever.

XVI.

But it takes the heart from out me,
    That deep confiding strain,
And I must beguile a little while
    Till it come back again.

Watton, 1844.

ODE ON THE THIRD CENTENARY OF THE ANNUAL COMMEMORATION IN TRINITY COLLEGE.

How sweep they by so fast
Those chariot-wheels of Time!
On, onward, swifter than the wintry blast
Athwart a wintry clime:
On, on—another hundred years
Pass'd, like a dream o' the night.
There is no space for mirth, no time for tears,
The swift hours sleep not in their flight,
The rivers pause not, and the mighty spheres
Still track their course of everlasting light.
Yet touch thy harp-strings, minstrel: let the throng
Sweep heedlessly along:

Pause, and with thoughtful spirits cast thine eye
Across the mighty regions left behind;
For spots lie there eternally enshrined,
    And hours that will not die.

    Another hundred years,
    From yonder sacred pile ;
The chime this day hath fallen on our ears
  To bid us gather in that holy aisle,
Where once our fathers gather'd : they have gone
  To their long home : and we, a little while,
Forth issuing from the cloud, speed on
Across the narrow twilight bridge, that lies
  Betwixt two vast eternities,
    Then hasten underneath
    The second cloud of death,
That skirts the confines where our fathers are,
A land that is so nigh, and seems so far.
They must not pass without a tear away,
  We must not live without deep thoughts of them ;
The mists are transient as the summer day,
  But stars live on in Heaven's great diadem,

Thrice have a hundred years pass'd by
These sacred walls, deepens the echoing cry.
　　And countless visions sweep
　　O'er fancy's startled sleep,
　Of fields of glory, wreaths of fame,
　And victories won on stormy seas,
　And many a warrior's spotless name—
　　Ay, nobler deeds than these.
Heroes, who fought, but for no earthly crown ;
Who fell, but ask'd of mortals no renown ;
Who dared to combat for their country's God,
　And for their God and country dared to die :
Their blood sank deep into the country's sod,
　Who weeps too late their martyr'd memory.
　　And still is seen the holy mien
　　Of England's great free-hearted Queen ;
And still is heard the waves' exuberant roar
Casting the Armada's wrecks in sport upon the shore.

　　How sweep they by so fast
　　　Those chariot-wheels of Time !
　　The echoes of the centuries are pass'd,
　　　Like a faint vesper chime.

Yet stormful was the cry,
And loud the thunder as they grated by :
  The crash of arms, the battle's groan ;
And shatter'd fell the sacred monarch's throne ;
And from her limbs imprison'd Freedom tore
Her fetters with a maniac's rage and roar :
  Till listening to the voice of truth
  She taught her proud heart gentler ruth :
Till o'er a freeborn race of faithful kings
Heaven waved triumphantly its guardian wings.

  The scene is changed once more :
Beneath a midnight lamp a student sits[1],
And muses oft long while, or reads by fits
  Pages of human lore :
  Then turns his ardent reverent look
  To Nature's greater nobler book,
Where from their deep blue homes on high
The stars greet meekly his meek eye,
  Interpreting the lines
  Of those mysterious signs,
All dimly traced upon the awful sky.

[1] Sir Isaac Newton.

New visions still crowd on, and memory tells

    Of glorious deeds of old,

    And many a patriot's name,

    But bound by mightier spells

We see them glide beneath the vaporous fold

Of the great past, nor linger o'er their fame :

    Though oft, in evening's twilight dews,

    We fondly love to muse,

    That whilome those high sages' feet

    Here humbly trode this still retreat,

    And learn'd to bend a childlike ear

To the low voice of heavenly wisdom here.

    How sweep they by so fast

    Those chariot-wheels of Time !

Leaving so brief a track of glories past,

    And hurrying on to crime.

    Have orphan'd children cried[2] ?

    Have captive daughters pined ?

    Have groans, ere now, been cast aside

    Unto the pitiless wind ?

[2] The Revolution of 1789.

Have dark clouds pass'd on the stormy blast?
    Darker are behind.
  They gather'd long, they lower'd low;
    All men trembling stood:
  They shed a few first drops of woe,
    At length they burst in blood!
    On smiling France at first,
    On guilty France they burst,
Her sainted monarch fell, her princes fled,
Her noblest, best, were number'd with the dead.
  In dungeon gloom her maidens' bloom
    Was counted cheap as dust;
And the innocent child there only smiled
    In its young unguarded trust.
    Wealth, beauty, talent died,
    And the rivers ran with gore;
Thou hast drunk the blood of thy choicest pride,
    Proud France!—and wilt have more?
The tempest hath not pass'd: the clouds of wrath
Sweep on enfolding in their awful gloom
All lands, Despair before their path;
  Behind, the silence of the tomb.

I see them form; I see them rise;
  Fainter grows the light;
Till they enshroud the glorious skies,
  And liken day to night.
And beneath are the dusty plains of war,
The steed, and the warrior's brazen car,
The lightning sword, and the cannon's shock,
And the rifle's rattle on rifted rock.

      And ever and anon
      A lull in the storm steals on:
      We listen—it is gone.

See yonder man with the eagle-eye,
And the soul that dares to do or die!
And his armies sweep from sea to sea,
And he tramples the proud, and enchains the free,
Till the earth at his fury stood aghast,
And the nations shook at his tread as he pass'd.

    Desolate—desolate—the wild flood
    Hath torn from the forest branch and leaf:
    And Europe is weeping tears of blood:—
      He sheds no tear of grief.
    But there is love in heaven: and angels weep
      If men forbear o'er human sufferings:

And freedom's cry, awaking from her sleep,

  In the proud conqueror's ear a death-knell rings.

He fell: and, moated by the chafing waves,

For whom all earth had seem'd too small a throne,

For whom unnumber'd myriads had sunk down

    Into untimely graves,

Slept in his narrow bed full tranquilly

Long silent years beneath the willow-tree.

  Touch, minstrel, touch thy lyre again

  To livelier music, for thy lay

Hath been in somewhat mournful solemn strain

    For a bright festal day.

What if the world's arena hath been rife

With sounds of discord, and fell deeds of strife,—

Here they have been as echoes faint and far;

  Here glide unruffled on the silent hours;

Peace dwells with Wisdom; and the evening star

  Shines ever cloudless o'er these sacred towers.

  What, though the tempest often sweep

  Recklessly o'er the billowy deep,—

This quiet crystal fountain hath flow'd on,

Shelter'd from every storm that raves anon,

And sent its copious floods
To gladden and renew on every hand
The valleys, and the wild banks, and the woods
    Of our great Fatherland.

And might I twine one parting wreath for thee,
    Dear college home, by thousand memories dear,
    Ere I forsake thy tranquil shores, and steer
To the bleak pathways of the trackless sea,
'Twere only adding to the debt I owe
    Of thanks, and gratitude, and filial love;
And faint my strains, and feeble were, and low,
    To tell thy worth, all praise of mine above.
Nay, rather, grateful prayers shall rise, that He,
    Beneath whose favouring smile
Thou art the glory of our native isle,
May ever shield, and guard, and prosper thee.
    Ours only be the joy to know,
    When in the world tost to and fro,
We once were shelter'd underneath thy walls,
O fairest, noblest, best of Granta's glorious halls.

Trinity College, 1846.

SONNET.

THERE's music on the winds: and far aloft
It sinks and rises as they rise and sink.
And evermore, like waters from the brink
Of over-joyful springs, in tones most soft
And most melodious, came quick bursts of song,
Like harpers harping on their harps: and oft
They fill'd my soul with worship; till among
The caverns of the clouds they seem'd to lose
The magic of their music: none might choose
But hear: the fount was rapture; and to drink,
A joy past utterance: and the morning dews
Chased mist-like the blue ocean waves along,
Till clouds, winds, waters, music-built did seem,
The shadows of an everlasting dream.

NOT LUCK, BUT LOVE.

[ON HEARING ANOTHER SPEAK OF LUCK.]

Not luck : though drifting to and fro
Chances and changes come and go ;
Though joys are broken lights empearl'd
On wild waves of this troublous world ;
Though unsuspected griefs and woes
Rise, ere a whisper whence they rose ;
Though oft the crystal morning-light
Is dark with tempest long ere night ;
Though smiles and tears are driven away,
Like sun and cloud some April day ;
Though hopes elate, or fears appall,—
Not luck, but Love is over all.

1870.

"LORD, SAVE ME."

" A RUIN'D sinner, lost, undone,—Lord Jesu, hear my cry:
The brand of guilt is on my soul; Lord, save me, or I die."
" I will, thou wreck'd and ruin'd one: before thee, lo, I stand;
Upon my bosom throw thyself, and grasp my pierced hand.
I will not spurn thee from my side for all thy rags and
    chains,
I love thee;—come to me, and wash thy dark and crimson
    stains."

" Ten thousand talents, Lord, I owe,—nothing have I to pay;
I dare not come, whose nakedness would shame the light of
    day."
" Come unto me, thou bankrupt soul; why dost thou linger
    yet ?
With my own life-blood I have paid the last mite of thy
    debt.

                                              o

My wealth, my goodness, give I thee, and, for thy ro;
    dress,

Will clothe thee with a seamless robe, my perfect rig]
    cousness."

" I fain would come, I fain would pray, my tears alone m₁
    speak;

I come;—yet seems my strengthless heart too wayward a
    too weak."

" I come to thee, come thou to me, thou weary one, a
    rest ;

And my meek Spirit shall abide within thy troubl
    breast.

His life and love, His power and peace, His majesty a
    might,

Are with thee ; listen to His voice; He speaks, and there
    light."

" I come, He draws me ; I am thine, Lord Jesu, Thou ɛ
    mine.

I ask no more, if only thus upon me Thou wilt shine."

"My Father loves thee, and I love ; my Spirit dwells in
    thee :
Herein is life, and joy, and heaven, and immortality.
But haply clouds will come, and hide thy Saviour from
    thine eyes ;
Say, wilt thou love me on beneath those future wintry
    skies ?"

"I only cast me on Thee, Lord ; I love Thee, though
    unseen ;
But when shall this dividing veil be raised that hangs
    between ?"
"Press onward, ransom'd one, press on to that celestial
    realm :
The voyage may be rough and long, but I am at the helm :
The wilderness is void and vast; but, see, I go before
    thee :
The battle may be fierce ; but I lead on before to glory."

"And shall I never leave Thy side upon that blissful shore,
But see Thee in Thy glorious home, and love Thee ever-
    more ?"

" For ever—thou shalt share my throne, my Father's face
behold,

And swell the rapturous melodies of thousand harps of
gold,

Fear not, for I will greet thee with my well-remember'd
smile :

Press on, be faithful unto death—'tis but a little while."

Hinton Martell, 1853.

THE WORLD'S PEACE, AND CHRIST'S.

TWO REAL INCIDENTS.

" Peace I leave you, my peace I give unto you; not as the world giveth,
give I unto you. Let not your heart be troubled, neither let it be
afraid."—John xiv. 27.

A CLOUDLESS sky—a laughing summer day—
   A river gliding noiselessly and deep—
Moor'd by whose brink a little shallop lay ;
   Within, two weary travellers asleep.
   Ha ! the boat loosens, and begins to sweep
With those strong waters to their headlong fall :
   The slumberers waken not, nor cry, nor weep ;
It strikes—they start astonied—one wild call,
One struggle, and the tide rolls onward burying all.

      *   *   *   *

A wintry ocean—a dark, rock-bound coast,
    And breakers whitening near—a shatter'd sail—
A vessel battling onward, tempest-toss'd:
    Aboard,—quick, hurrying footsteps, and the wail
    Of women, and brave men in silence pale.
One only, with a calm, untroubled eye,
    Watch'd the wild waters and the wilder gale—
The pilot's playful child; and, question'd why,
"My father's at the helm," was her untaught reply.

Hinton Martell, 1853.

THE THRESHOLD OF THINGS UNSEEN.

I.

THE BABE'S FIRST JOURNEY.

[Baby sleeps while the angel soars heavenward, singing.]

" My treasure, my blossom,

    My blessing twice bless'd,

Folded close to my bosom,

    Be still and at rest.

Winds and waters were rougher

    Than wonted at last,

But no more shalt thou suffer,

    No more—it is pass'd.

Not a sigh, not a sorrow

    Shall grieve thee to-night,

And the dawn of to-morrow

    Is cloudless delight."

[*Baby, half-waking, half-sleeping, lisps its first words in the language of heaven.*]

"O mother, dear mother,
    Who is this? where am I?"

[*The angel continues singing.*]

"Thy guardian, thy brother:
    Fear not, I am nigh.
See the star-lamps adorning
    This beautiful dome;
See the smile of the morning;
    I am bearing thee home.
Mansions there without number
    For infants are built;
Awake from thy slumber,
    Awake, if thou wilt."

[*Baby catches the first glimpse of heaven, and asks,—*]

"Oh, what is that glory
    That shines on thy wings?
Brother, tell me a story
    Of heavenly things."

[*The angel sings on.*]

" There joy without measure,
  There day without night,
And rivers of pleasure
  Shall break on thy sight.
There are gold paths transparent
  And gateways of pearl;
There the babe and the parent,
  The boy and the girl,
With angels, are walking
  And plucking the fruit,
And singing or talking
  To sound of the lute.
No shadows can darken
  Their blessed employ:
Hush, baby, and hearken
  The sound of their joy.
See, the Lord of the garden
  Our coming awaits."

*   *   *   *

So the babe and its warden
  Pass'd in at the gates,

And stronger and stronger
        The glory became;
    And I saw them no longer:
        I woke from my dream.

1864.

————◆————

II.

THE CHILD'S HOME-CALL.

A FACT.

"And was carried by the angels into Abraham's bosom."—LUKE xvi. 22.

My eyes are very dim, mother,
        I cannot see you right;
    Sit near, and read my favourite hymn,
        For I shall die to-night.

    "Jesus who lived,"—yes, that, mother,
        I learn'd it on your knee;
    Well I remember where you sate,
        When first you taught it me.

Oh, yes, read on and on, mother,
The words that Jesus said:
And think, long after I am gone,
He bore our sins instead.

Is the rush-candle out, mother?
For all is midnight dark;
Oh, take my hand—I will not doubt:
See mother—mother, hark!

Oh, bright and blessed things, mother,
My soul it is that sees;
Yet feel you not the rush of wings
Makes musical the breeze?

Kind faces throng the room, mother,
And gentle loving eyes:
Do you not hear, " Come, sister, come,"
My welcome to the skies?

Is this the happy land, mother?
My heart is almost still.—
The childless mother felt her hand
All in a moment chill.

Banningham, 1851.

III.

TRANSLATED, NOT CONFIRMED.

TO ONE WHO WITH ME WATCHED THE PARTING HOURS OF
A CANDIDATE FOR CONFIRMATION.

TOGETHER we leant
    O'er her fragile form,
As her head she bent
    To the long last storm.

There was nothing of fear
    In that dying room,
For Jesus was near
    And chased its gloom.

We ask'd if she felt
    His presence was nigh,
And the deep answer dwelt
    In her up-lighted eye.

" Have you cast on His cross
    The weight of your sin ?

Is the world but loss ?
　　Is there peace within ?"

On the calm of that hour,
　　Why further press,
When we knew the power
　　Of her gentle " Yes" ?

She is gone—as a child
　　On its mother's breast ;
She look'd up, and smiled,
　　And sank to rest.

The waves are all pass'd,
　　The word has been given,
Though roughest at last,
　　They have borne her to heaven.

But "a little while,"
　　And our summons will come—
Oh, then with her smile
　　To ascend to her home !

Tunbridge Wells, 1852.

IV.

THE PENITENT'S DEATH-BED.

"As many as touched the hem of His garment were made perfectly
whole."

A COLD and wild autumnal sky: the sun was sinking fast,

And bleakly blew o'er wood and wold the wintry northern
blast;

The chill rain fell in sudden gusts, still drifting on and on,

The day had pass'd in storms, and night would now be
here anon.

Around the far horizon's skirts despairing roved the eye,

When lo! a rainbow-fragment stamp'd upon that stormy
sky.

Broken and quivering it lay, one little fragment given

From some few flickering beams of light far in the western
heaven:

The trembling colours came and went, and fainter, brighter
grew

Amid that wild untender sky, so tender and so true.

I just had left the dying bed of one who once had been

A wanderer from the Saviour's fold in the gloomy paths of
    sin—

A wreck of sweetness and of grace, a shade of beauty
    now,

Though Death had set its awful seal too plainly on her
    brow.

Oh, surely life to her had been a life of guilt and tears,

Of blighted hopes and shatter'd dreams, and storms of
    guilty fears !

But, on a sudden, in the midst of youth and pleasure's
    prime,

The icy blast of death blew keen athwart that summer
    clime.

The world's allurements shrivell'd then, like leaves in wind
    and frost,

And all its lying blandishments their sometime glory
    lost.

Earth trembled, and the sky was gloom, and all within
    was wild,

And death full quickly now would claim its own unhappy
    child.

Stay, list!—a sudden ray from heaven gleam'd in upon
  her cell:

"The Saviour"—eagerly she caught the accents as they
  fell—

"The Saviour came to save the lost—Jesus for sinners
  died."

"For sinners?—Oh, the worst am I of sinners," she re-
  plied.

"Then cast on Him thy load of guilt—He bids thee come
  and live."

"I cannot, yet I would," she cried; "Lord, hear me, Lord,
  forgive!"

It was not peace, it was not light, nor was it all despair,
And pointing her to Jesus still, I left her after prayer.
It was not sunshine, nor the joy of heaven's own glorious
  bow,
Yet surely one true little gleam of mercy amid woe,—
One fragmentary rainbow-spot that might grow brighter
  yet,
And faintly promised better things before the sun was set.

Banningham, 1848.

V.

IS IT WELL?

NEVER man spake like Him.   His words of power
Fell like the healing dews of heaven.   His looks
Breathed love: and round Him eagerly there press'd
The sick in body and the sick at heart.
Some clung in painful anguish to His hand;
Some cast themselves before His sacred feet;   •
Some cried aloud for mercy; and His grace
Was free to all.   He cast out none who came.
But some there were of timid trembling faith,
Who stole behind Him in the press, and touch'd
The border of His garment; and there went
Such virtue from Him, all who touch'd were heal'd.
The feeblest touch was life.   And He is still
Unchangeably, eternally the same.

Then weep not for thy well-beloved, nor ask
Mistrustful, "Is it well with him I mourn?"
Was he not clinging to the Saviour's hand?

P

Was he not holding to the Saviour's feet?

Was he not hanging on the Saviour's grace?

Is love still anxious?   Laid he not his finger

Upon the border of the Saviour's robe?

That trembling touch was everlasting life.

1863.

━━━━◆━━━

VI.

THE UNKNOWN TO-MORROW.

So he is gone: it was but yesterday

He spent in piloting his cumbrous car

Through crowds of men and tangled thoroughfares

Of this great city.   Evening came, and night;

And having done his duty he return'd,

Worn out and weary, to his quiet home.

There the sweet love of wife, a daughter's care,

The soft low breath of younger children sleeping,

And thoughts, that wander'd to his absent boy,

Refresh'd him.   On his knees he sank in prayer,

Short, earnest, true,—and laid him down to rest.

It was his last day's work.   Where is he now?

Where is he?   Suddenly the message came;

And angels bare him on their wings of love

Into his Saviour's presence.   No more toil;

No more the din and discord of the world;

No more the weary warfare of the heart.

He sleeps in Jesus: on his head a crown

Of glory; in his hand a harp of praise;

And music of the blessed spirits, who walk

The golden streets, about him echoing joy

And welcoming another traveller home.

1863.

VII.

THE THREE BIRTHDAYS.

TO THE MEMORY OF ONE WHO, IN BLINDNESS AND SUFFERING, BUT
IN THE FULL ASSURANCE OF FAITH, SAID, A FEW HOURS BEFORE
HER DEATH, THAT SHE HAD ALWAYS HEARD THAT THREE BIRTH-
DAYS WERE OURS:—OUR NATURAL BIRTHDAY, OUR SPIRITUAL
BIRTHDAY, AND OUR BIRTHDAY INTO GLORY: AND THAT SHE
WAS SURE THE LAST WAS THE BRIGHTEST AND THE BEST.

Joy for thee, newborn child of heaven! once there was joy
        on earth,

What time from eager lip to lip ran tidings of thy birth,

And glad hearts beat more gladly, and quick steps more
  quickly trod
To tell that home was richer with another gift from God.

Years fleeted by; until beneath the brooding of the Dove,
Thy heart was warm'd and waken'd to the voice of hea-
  venly love;
Then deeper waves of joy across their golden harp-strings
  stole,
As angels sang before the throne the birthday of thy soul.

Years fleeted by; and still thy path grew brighter and more
  bright,
And stars from daylight hidden gemm'd the clear sky of
  thy night.
Thy spirit drank of rivulets that never could run dry;
And suffering never seem'd to cloud the summer of thy sky.

And all who knew thee loved thee; and they loved thee
  most of all,
Who mark'd thy patient waiting for thy Master's long'd-for
  call:

It came, at last, that joy of joys, the latest and the best,
The birthday of a child of heaven,—the dawn of perfect rest

Dear sainted sister, we rejoice, the more we weep our loss;
And while we think upon thy crown, more humbly bear ou
    cross.
For in our heart of hearts is heard the calm propheti
    warning,
The bridal of the Church is near, her glory's natal mornin

1861.

DEATH AND VICTORY.

THOU speakest of the fear of death, its ghastliness and
    gloom,
And dreary shadows flung across the portals of the tomb ;
Thou sayest that the best of men must tremble like the
    grass,
When from the loved and lovely earth to unknown worlds
    they pass :
Thou picturest the love of home, the light of childhood's
    sky,
And askest, Who could leave such things with no heart-
    breaking sigh ?

My heart was pain'd ; and oft I thought, Can this be true
    of those
Who have on Jesus cast the guilt and burden of their
    woes ?—

Till, as I mused, the truths of God, like beacon-fires at
    night,

Gleam'd forth from Scripture's vivid page upon my aching
    sight :—

"I know that my Redeemer lives; and, though my flesh
    must die,

By dying He shall swallow up the grave in victory.

Ay, in the shadowy vale of death no evil will I fear,

For Thou art with me, Thou, my God, to animate and cheer."

So sang the patriarchs of old, before the veil was riven.

Which from the pilgrim fathers hid the open gate of
    heaven :

But hark, what clearer tidings now our songs of triumph
    swell !

" Christ Jesus hath abolish'd death, and holds the keys of
    hell ;

He lives, and whoso trusts in Him shall never, never die;

He lives,—this mortal shall be clothed with immortality.

The portals of the tomb are burst ; ye ransom'd captives, sing,

Where is thy victory, O Grave? where, darksome Death,
    thy sting ?"

No wild dreams these,—I speak of things that oftentimes
    have been ;

Of parting words that I have heard, and death-beds I have
    seen ;

Of a long-loved father, circled by his children and his wife,

With every joy to gladden earth, and bind him unto life,

Who calmly said, " My children must not stay me from my
    rest ;

My work is finish'd, and I long to sleep on Jesus' breast ;

Death cannot part me from His love—Lord Jesu, it is
    Thou—

I have no fear, my children ; for my Lord is with me now."

And gentle girls, too, have I seen, who seem'd for earth too
    frail,

Tread with a firm confiding step, adown that lonesome vale;

Ay, and on childhood's pallid lip have words of triumph
    play'd,

And tiny fingers, clasp'd in death, told, " I am not afraid."

But why speak on of scenes like these, when every heart
    must know

Some parent, partner, brother, child, who trembled not to go

Where Jesus' steps had gone before, and He himself is nigh,
Whispering above those boisterous waves, "Fear nothing,
 it is I"?

Ours is the grief, who still are left in this far wilderness,
Which will at times, now they are gone, seem blank and
 comfortless.
For moments spent with loving hearts are breezes from the
 hills,
And the balm of Christian brotherhood like Eden's dew
 distils:
And we whose footsteps and whose hearts so often fail and
 faint,
Seem ill to spare the cheering voice of one departed saint.

But oh, we sorrow not like those whom no bright hopes
 sustain,
For them who sleep in Jesus, God will with Him bring again.
Love craves the presence and the sight of all its well-
 beloved,
And therefore weep we in the homes whence they are far
 removed;

Love craves the presence and the sight of each beloved one,

And therefore Jesus spake the word which caught them
  to His throne :—

" Father, I will that all my own, which Thou hast granted
  Me,

Be with Me where I am to share my glory's bliss with
  Thee."

Thus heaven is gathering, one by one, in its capacious
  breast,

All that is pure and permanent, and beautiful and blest ;

The family is scatter'd yet, though of one home and heart,

Part militant in earthly gloom, in heavenly glory part.

But who can speak the rapture, when the circle is complete,

And all the children sunder'd now around one Father meet ?

One fold, one Shepherd, one employ, one everlasting home :

" Lo! I come quickly."   " Even so, Amen !   Lord Jesu,
  come !"

1851

. THE TROUBLE OF JESUS' SOUL.

John xii. 27.

"And now is my soul troubled."   Can it be?
O speak the word again, and yet again.
Thy soul, O holy Saviour, troubled?   Peace,
Be comforted, my weak and weary heart:
There is a deep unfathomable rest
In that low moan of anguish.   Was Thy soul,
O Jesu, troubled, tempest-tost, like mine?—
Troubled?—Thy faith held fast her anchor-hold
Upon the Rock of everlasting strength:
For Thee the light of coming glory shone
Beyond all clouds, that wrapp'd the vale of death:
It was Thy daily meat and drink to do
Thy Father's will, which in Thy secret breast

Was ever springing up a well of life,
The world knew nothing of.   And yet Thy soul
Was troubled.

           Trouble then was uppermost,
Not joy, not peace, but trouble and unrest,
What time these holy words dropp'd from Thy lips:
There was no stain of sin in them, no film
Of evil; only grief, deep sinless grief,
As when a tempest scourges into waves
A calm and crystal lake.

               Oh, peace, my heart:
It is not sin to feel the bitterness
Of sorrow, nor to tremble, as the storm
Rocks the foundations of our little all:
It is not sin to weep, and make our moan.
Nay, for this human suffering Jesus felt,
And wept, and shudder'd, and confess'd His woe;
Though almost in the self-same breath of prayer
He pleaded, " Father, glorify Thy name,"
And meekly bow'd His head to bear the cross.

I thank Thee, Lord, for these Thy words of grief;
I thank Thee more for Thy victorious love:
So teach me at Thy feet to kneel and learn,
Until my feeble prayer re-echoes Thine,
" Father, Thy will, not mine, Thy will be done."

1862.

NO MORE CRYING.

REV. xxi. 4.

I LAY upon my bed, and dream'd a dream.
Time and its conflicts had, methought, long since
Been number'd with the past.   Nothing was heard
But Hallelujahs from the universe:
Our Father's will was done, His kingdom come:
Earth was a nursery for heaven.   When, lo!
Among the mingled ranks of saints and seraphs
Who stood before the throne, a short sharp cry—
A short, sharp, passionate cry—suddenly rose:
One cry, and from the humblest of that throng;
One little cry, and in a moment hush'd.
But instantly the glorious tide of praise,
Which for long ages had flow'd on and on

In ever-deepening waves of crystal joy,

Was troubled. Angel on archangel look'd

Amazed, abash'd, appall'd: saint gazed on saint

Incredulous: and quickly through all worlds

The sympathetic tidings spread dismay.

Wherefore? Was heaven's felicity so frail?

Whence had that cry such terrors? Sin, sin, sin:

Faint, feeble, fugitive; but real sin.

Had Satan broken loose? Should evil cast

Again its dismal shadow over good?

Angels grew pale; all faces gather'd gloom;

Thunders began to roll. And with the shock

I woke; and waking knew it was a dream,

A feverish nightmare-dream, earth-born, earth-bred,

And one of heaven's impossibilities.

1867.

Hymns.

THE PRINCE OF PEACE.

I.

HARK, hark! the advent cry again:
 The angels sing His birth,
"Glory to God, goodwill to men,
  And peace on earth."

II.

He comes; and eager listeners throng
 The lowly path He trod;
For peace is ever on His tongue,—
  The peace of God.

III.

See, His frail bark the waters fill:
 Yet why that faithless dread?
Before His mighty "Peace, be still,"
  The storm is fled.

IV.

A weeping sinner dares to touch
    And bathe His feet with tears :
And " Go in peace: thou lovest much,"
    Is all she hears.

V.

His hour is come: sad bosoms heave
    With bodings unexpress'd:
Peace—grief itself forgets to grieve
    At His bequest.

VI.

O never, never, gentle Dove,
    Let Thy soft pleadings cease,
Until we bask in light, and love,
    And perfect peace.

1869.

Q

THE ROCK OF AGES.

"Thou art the same, and Thy years shall have no end."
—Ps. cii. 27.

O GOD, the Rock of Ages,
  Who evermore hast been,
What time the tempest rages,
  Our dwelling-place serene :
Before Thy first creations,
  O Lord, the same as now,
To endless generations
  The Everlasting Thou !

Our years are like the shadows
  On sunny hills that lie,
Or grasses in the meadows
  That blossom but to die :

A sleep, a dream, a story
By strangers quickly told,
An unremaining glory
Of things that soon are old.

O Thou, who canst not slumber,
Whose light grows never pale,
Teach us aright to number
Our years before they fail.
On us Thy mercy lighten,
On us Thy goodness rest,
And let Thy Spirit brighten
The hearts Thyself hast bless'd.

Lord, crown our faith's endeavour
With beauty and with grace,
Till, clothed in light for ever,
We see Thee face to face:
A joy no language measures;
A fountain brimming o'er;
An endless flow of pleasures;
An ocean without shore.

1862.

THE HIDING-PLACE.

"A man shall be as an hiding-place from the wind and a covert from the tempest, as rivers of water in a dry place, as the shadow of a great rock in a weary land."—Isa. xxxii. 2.

O Jesu, Saviour of the lost,
    My rock and hiding-place;
By storms of sin and sorrow tost
    I seek Thy sheltering grace.

Guilty, forgive me, Lord, I cry;
    Pursued by foes I come;
A sinner, save me, or I die;
    An outcast,—take me home.

Once safe in Thine Almighty arms,
    Let storms come on amain;
There danger never, never harms,
    There death itself is gain.

And when I stand before Thy throne,

    And all Thy glory see;

Still be my righteousness alone,

    To hide myself in Thee.

1850.

"ABIDE IN ME."

JOHN xv. 4.

"ABIDE in Me, and I in you:"
  Ah, blessed, sweet commands;
Soft as the fall of early dew,
  On parched, thirsty lands.

Abide in Thee, my Lord, my God,
  Omnipotent to save
From all the dangers of my road,
  From Satan and the grave.

In Thee, whose wisdom none can tell,
  Whose grace no limit knows;
Whose love divine, unsearchable,
  A boundless ocean flows.

Then welcome joy, and farewell fear,
    And calm, ye wild waves, be;
If only, Lord, Thy voice I hear,
    "My child, abide in Me."

1849.

HYMN TO THE HOLY TRINITY.

"Who shall not fear Thee, O Lord, and glorify Thy name?"—
REV. xv. 4.

FATHER of heaven above,
Dwelling in light and love,
 Ancient of days,
Light unapproachable,
Love inexpressible,
Thee, the Invisible,
 Laud we and praise.

Christ, the eternal Word,
Christ, the incarnate Lord,
 Saviour of all,
High throned above all height,
God of God, Light of Light,
Increate, infinite,
 On Thee we call.

O God, the Holy Ghost,
Whose fires of Pentecost
   Burn evermore,
In this far wilderness
Leave us not comfortless:
Thee we love, Thee we bless,
   Thee we adore.

Strike your harps, heavenly powers;
With your glad chants shall ours
   Trembling ascend:
All praise, O God, to Thee,
Three in One, One in Three,
Praise everlastingly,
   World without end.

1870.

THE TRUMPET OF JUBILEE.

"Trumpets of silver."—NUM. x. 2.

O BROTHERS, lift your voices,
 Triumphant songs to raise ;
Till heaven on high rejoices,
 And earth is fill'd with praise.
Ten thousand hearts are bounding
 With holy hopes, and free ;
The Gospel trump is sounding,
 The trump of Jubilee.

O Christian brothers ! glorious
 Shall be the conflict's close :
The cross hath been victorious,
 And shall be o'er its foes.

Faith is our battle-token ;
　　Our Leader all controls ;
Our trophies, fetters broken ;
　　Our captives, ransom'd souls.

Not unto us—Lord Jesus,
　　To Thee all praise be due !
Whose blood-bought mercy frees us,
　　Has freed our brethren too.
Not unto us—in glory
　　The angels catch the strain,
And cast their crowns before Thee
　　Exultingly again.

Captain of our salvation,
　　Thy presence we adore :
Praise, glory, adoration
　　Be Thine for evermore !
Still on in conflict pressing
　　On Thee Thy people call,
Thee, King of kings, confessing,
　　Thee crowning Lord of all.

1849.

"HE SHALL GATHER THE LAMBS WITH HIS ARM."

Isaiah xl. 11.

Poor shepherdless lambs, amid darkness and dangers,
    We sported in paths of temptation and sin ;
We had heedlessly follow'd the bidding of strangers,
    None guided us out, and none folded us in.

But Jesus heard tell of our pitiful story,
    And love fill'd His bosom with grief for our loss,
For us He forsook the bright mansions of glory,
    And came to the manger, the garden, the cross.

He sought and He found: in His bosom He laid us,
    And show'd us the marks in His hands and His feet,
And gently, meanwhile, to His sheepfold convey'd us,
    A shelter from tempest, a shadow from heat.

With His crook and His staff He doth govern and guide
    us :
How green are the pastures, the waters how clear !
While Jesus is with us, what harm shall betide us ?
    While He is our shepherd, what foe shall we fear ?

'Tis true that in places the path may be thorny ;
    And of the dark valley He us has foretold ;
But He promises He will go all the long journey,
    And bring us safe through to His heavenly fold.

He says, be the path thither longer or shorter,
    No cloud ever darkens our home in the skies ;
For He'll lead us beside living fountains of water,
    And God shall wipe off every tear from our eyes.

1850.

BAPTISM OF SUCH AS ARE OF RIPER YEARS.

" And now, why tarriest thou ?   Arise, and be baptized, and wash a
thy sins, calling on the name of the Lord."—ACTS xxii. 16.

STAND, soldier of the cross,
Thy high allegiance claim,
And vow to hold the world but loss
For thy Redeemer's name.

Arise, and be baptized,
And wash thy sins away:
Thy faith and hope be realized,
Thy love avouch'd to-day.

Our heavenly country now,
Our Lord and Master, thine,
Receive imprinted on thy brow
His Passion's awful sign.

No more thine own, but Christ's;
With all the saints of old,
Apostles, seers, evangelists,
And martyr throngs enroll'd,—

In God's whole armour strong,
Front hell's embattled powers:
The warfare may be sharp and long,
The victory must be ours.

O bright the conqueror's crown,
The song of triumph sweet,
When faith casts every trophy down
At our Great Captain's feet.

1870.

CONFIRMATION HYMN.

[To be sung after the benedictory prayer, " Defend, O Lord, this Thy
ervant with Thy heavenly grace, that he may continue Thine for
ever," &c.]

" I am Thine, save me."—Ps. cxix. 94.

" THINE, Thine for ever "—blessed bond
    That knits us, Lord, to Thee:
May voice, and heart, and soul respond
    Amen, so let it be.

When this world strikes its dulcet harp,
    And earth our heaven appears,
Be " Thine for ever," clear and sharp,
    God's trumpet in our ears.

When sin in pleasure's soft disguise
   Would work us deadliest harm,
May "Thine for ever" from the skies
   Steal down, and break the charm.

When Satan flings his fiery darts
   Against our weary shield,
May "Thine for ever" in our hearts
   Forbid us faint or yield.

Thine all along the flowery spring,
   · Along the summer prime,
Till autumn fades in welcoming
   The silver frost of time.

"Thine, Thine for ever"—body, soul,
   Henceforth devote to thee,
While everlasting ages roll :
   Amen, so let it be.

1870.

R

REST IN THE LORD: MARRIAGE HYMN.

" Rest in the Lord."—Ps. xxxvii. 7.

Rest in the Lord—from harps above
The music seems to thrill—
Rest in His everlasting love,
    Rest and be still.

Rest thou, who claimest for thine own
Thy chosen bride to-day,
Affianced in His faith alone
    Thy bride for aye.

And thou, whose trustful hand is given
Avouching here thy spouse,
Rest, for a Father seals in heaven
    His children's vows.

Rest ye, who cluster round them both
   To mingle praise and prayers;
Your God affirms the plighted troth,
    Your God and theirs.

Rest, for the Heavenly Bridegroom here
   Is standing by your side,
And in this union draws more near
    His mystic bride.

Rest in the Lord—thrice Holy Dove,
   In us Thy word fulfil—
Rest in His everlasting love,
    Rest and be still.

1869.

THE MARRIAGE BENEDICTION.

[To be sung after the blessing, "Almighty God, who at the beginning did create our first parents," &c.]

" Being heirs together of the grace of life."—1 PET. iii. 7.

ERE the words of peace and love,

Breathed on earth, are borne above,

While their echo, soft and clear,

Lingers on the trancèd ear,—

Catch upon your lips the strain,

Swell the notes of prayer again,

Prayer with benedictions fraught,

Passing words and passing thought:

> Co-eternal Three in One,
>
> Seal the nuptial benison.

Blessings from the earth beneath,

Fruits and flowers in woven wreath;

Balmy dews that heaven distils
On the everlasting hills;
Angel wings, a guard of light
O'er the peaceful home by night;
Angel steps to tend the way
Onward, heavenward, day by day:
    Co-eternal Three in One,
    Seal the nuptial benison.

Hear our prayer: this union be
Ratified, O God, by Thee;
This another link entwined
Hearts and homes and heaven to bind
In that mystic chain of love,
Holding us, but held above;
Knitting all that world to this,
Eden's bloom to glory's bliss:
    Co-Eternal Three in One,
    Seal the nuptial benison.

Three in One, and One in Three,
Blessedness is blessing Thee;

While we pour in chant and hymn

Full hearts, flowing o'er the brim,—

Water by Thy power benign

Blushing as celestial wine,—

Till within the golden gates,

Where the Lamb His bridal waits,

　　We with all the white-robed throngs

　　Sing the heavenly Song of Songs.

⁎ This Hymn may be most appropriately sung to the first tune (Air by Mendelssohn) assigned to No. 43, "Hark! the herald angels sing," in "Hymns Ancient and Modern."

1869.

THE VILLAGE EVENING HYMN.

"Strangers and pilgrims on the earth."—HEB. xi. 13.

HARK, the nightly church-bell numbers
  One day more with bygone things;
Saviour, o'er our peaceful slumbers
  Spread Thy everlasting wings.

One day less of sin and sadness,
  One day nearer heaven and home:
Travellers to light and gladness,
  Onward stage by stage we roam.

One day less of toil and labour,
  One day nearer rest, and Thee.
Child and parent, friend and neighbour,
  Lift your voice, and bend your knee.

Blessed Spirit, hover o'er us,
　　Sleeping, waking, be Thou near;
Comrades, there is joy before us,
　　Rest in peace, and rise in prayer.

1853.

HYMN TO BE USED AT SEA.

"O God of our salvation, who art the confidence of them that are afar off upon the sea."—Ps. lxv. 5.

LORD of the ocean, hear our cry,
As o'er the trackless deep we roam;
Be Thou, our haven, always nigh;
On homeless waters Thou our home.

O Jesu, Saviour, at whose voice
The tempest sank to perfect rest,
Bid Thou the mourner's heart rejoice,
And cleanse and calm the troubled breast.

O Holy Ghost, beneath whose power
Creation woke to life and light,
Command Thy blessing in this hour,
Thy fostering warmth, Thy quickening might.

Great God, Triune Jehovah, Thee
We love, we worship, we adore;
Our refuge on time's changeful sea,
Our joy on heaven's eternal shore.

1869.

THE INSTITUTION OF THE LORD'S SUPPER.

"I will not drink henceforth of this fruit of the vine, until I drink it
new with you in my Father's kingdom."—MATT. xxvi. 29.

THE hour is come; the feast is spread:
    Behold My body given;
Behold My life-blood freely shed
    To ransom souls for heaven.

When of this cup I drink again,
    In glory and with you,
No tears its perfect joy shall stain,
    A joy for ever new.

Ere then ten thousand thousand times
    My table shall be spread,
And countless souls in distant climes
    Be comforted and fed.

Grace, mercy, peace be multiplied
   To those who commune there;
While seated by My Father's side
   Their mansion I prepare.

But now these lips a different cup
   For you must taste and drain,
And unrepiningly drink up
   The dregs of bitter pain.

The griefs ye know not that are Mine,
   Nor yet My glories see;
But break the bread, and drink the wine,
   And thus remember Me.

1850.

COMMUNION OF THE SICK.

"I sleep, but my heart waketh: it is the voice of my beloved that knocketh, saying, Open to me, my sister, my love, my dove, my undefiled: for my head is filled with dew, and my locks with the drops of the night."—SONG v. 2.

"Behold, I stand at the door, and knock: if any man hear my voice, and open the door, I will come in to him, and will sup with him, and he with me."—REV. iii. 20.

THE sun is set, the twilight's o'er,
　　The night dews fall like rain:
A Prince stands at a suppliant's door,
　　And knocks, and knocks again.

"I slumber; but my heart is moved
　　With joy and holy fear:
Is it Thy footstep, O beloved,
　　Thy hand, Thy voice I hear?"

" Tis I, thy Lord, who stand and wait
    Beneath the darkening sky:
Arise, unbar, unclose the gate,
    Fear nothing; it is I.

" The bread of life is in My hand;
    The wine of heaven I bring:
Fulfil My tenderest last command:
    Thy Bridegroom is thy King.

" Eat, drink; and muse in loving trust,
    The while I sup with thee,
If this be heaven on earth, what must
    My Bridal banquet be."

1869.

TILL HE COME.

"As often as ye eat this bread, and drink this cup, ye do show forth the Lord's death till He come."—1 Cor. xi. 26.

" TILL He come—" Oh, let the words
Linger on the trembling chords ;
Let the little while between
In their golden light be seen ;
Let us think how heaven and home
Lie beyond that 'Till He come.'

When the weary ones we love
Enter on their rest above,
Seems the earth so poor and vast,
All our life-joy overcast :
Hush, be every murmur dumb,
It is only—till He come.

Clouds and conflicts round us press :
Would we have one sorrow less ?
All the sharpness of the cross,
All that tells the world is loss,
Death, and darkness, and the tomb,
Only whisper, " Till He come."

See, the feast of love is spread,
Drink the wine, and break the bread,—
Sweet memorials,—till the Lord
Call us round His heavenly board ;
Some from earth, from glory some,
Sever'd only—till He come.

1861.

"HARPERS HARPING WITH THEIR HARPS."

REVELATION xiv. 2.

On the hill of Zion standing,
  Lo! the Lamb of God appears:
Scenes of glory far expanding
  Far above this vale of tears;
Songs of rapture, falling sweet on mortal ears.

Lo! He comes! with awful wonder
  Hark, those strains of joy untold;
Deepening on and on like thunder
  Never learnt or sung of old:
Blissful harpers, harping on their harps of gold.

s

Lo! He comes! in heaven appearing,

Mark yon herald angel's flight,

Glad eternal tidings bearing

To the lands of heathen night.

O'er the nations breaks a flood of Gospel light.

Lo! He comes! the heavens unfold Him ;

King of Kings, He comes to reign ;

Crown'd, enthroned, ye saints, behold Him.

Once for you baptized in pain.

Come, Lord Jesus!   Even so, Amen, Amen.

1849.

HE COMETH.

"Hallelujah : for the Lord God omnipotent reigneth."—REV. xix. 6.

HALLELUJAH ! He cometh with clouds and with light,
And the trumpet of God, in the silence of night:
Heaven's armies before Him adoringly bend,
And thousands of thousands His bidding attend.

Hallelujah ! He cometh : and every eye
Beholds Him with anguish or rapturous joy;
A wailing is heard from the kindreds of earth,
It is drown'd in Hosannas of heavenly mirth.

Hallelujah ! He cometh: the judgment is set,
And the nations are gather'd in crowds to His feet;
The earth and the ocean have yielded their dead,
And the records of time are unfolded and read.

s 2

Hallelujah! earth crumbles in ashes and dust,

While calmly He severs the wicked and just,

The shadows of darkness are driven away,

And the morning has dawn'd of eternal day.

1850.

THE WALK TO EMMAUS.

Slowly along the rugged pathway walk'd
Two sadden'd wayfarers, bent on one quest;—
With them Another who had ask'd to share
Their travel, since they left the city walls;—
Their converse too intent for speed: and oft,
Where linger'd on the rocks the sunset tints,
They check'd their footsteps, careless of the hour
And waning light and heavy falling dews.
For from the Stranger's lips came words, that burn'd
And lit the altar fuel on their hearts,
Consuming fear, and quickening faith at once.
God's oracles grew luminous as He spake;
And all along the ages Good from Ill
And light from darkness sprang, as day from night.

The first faint dawn from ruin'd Eden rose,

And glimmer'd round the solitary ark,

And lighted up Moriah's sacrifice,

And shed its warmth on Jacob's dying couch,

And bathed the blood-stained mercy-seat with love;

The Eastern heavens were flush'd with rosier gleams:

It woke the minstrel shepherd, and his hand,

Obedient to the gladness, struck his harp,

"Joy cometh in the morning;" and the words

Thereafter lived in song.   Isaiah's soul

Glow'd with the coming glory, and his page

Caught the far splendours of the orient clouds;

And plaintive Jeremy look'd up and smiled;

And rapt Ezekiel breathed his hopes in fire.

A deeper shade is glooming on the hills:

A livelier amber brightens in the sky

And broadens, till the Sun of Righteousness

Rises at last with healing in His wings.

Thus on their path they communed, till they reach'd

The lowly wicket, and their urgent plea,

" Day is far spent, abide with us," prevail'd.

The lamp is lighted o'er the simple board;

And there is silence for a space: but lo,
The Stranger takes the bread and blesses it
And breaks: and like a dream the veil is rent
Which hid their Lord and Master from their gaze.
It is His eye, His hand, His voice, Himself.
Fain had they fallen at His feet, and fain
Clung to Him as of old: it may not be;
His place is empty, but His love is there,
A calm abiding Presence in their hearts.

O Jesu, Saviour, hear our cry.   We too
Are weary travellers on life's rough path.
And Thou art still unchangeably the same.
Come, Lord, to us and let us walk with Thee:
Come and unfold the words of heavenly life,
Till our souls burn within us, and the day
Breaks, and the Day-star rises in our hearts.
Yea, Lord, abide with us, rending the veil
Which hides Thee from the loving eye of faith,
Dwell with us to the world's end evermore,
Until thou callest us to dwell with Thee.

1870.

THE THREE FOLLOWING POEMS

OBTAINED

THE CHANCELLOR'S MEDAL

AT THE CAMBRIDGE COMMENCEMENT, IN
THE YEARS 1844, 1845, 1846.

THE TOWER OF LONDON.

Αἴλινον, αἴλινον εἰπὲ, τὸ δ' εὖ νικάτω.

I.

I STOOD beside the waters—and at night—
  The voice of thousands now at last was still;
Silent the streets, and the wan moon's pale light
  Fell silently upon the waters chill.
  Ah! silence there—strange visions seem to fill
My desolate spirit—for I stood the last,
  I, the lone lingerer by the lonely hill:
The stars wept night-dews, and the fitful blast,
Whispering of other years, beside me moan'd and pass'd.

II.

I leant and mused.   Beneath the midnight sky,
    Stretch'd in dim outline, rose those turrets grey:
Like wave-worn monuments, where passers by
    Linger, and dream of ages pass'd away,
    They stood in silence.   Strangely wild were they ;
For Silence hath unto herself a spell:
    She hath a syren voice; and like the play
Of winds on crystal waters, she can tell
Of regions all her own, where dream-like fancies dwell.

III.

And led by her I dreamt, and saw, methought,
    The time when yonder waters roll'd between
No walls and granite turrets, but, untaught,
    Through the oak forest and the woodland green
    Flow'd, kissing every floweret.   Wild the scene:
For Britons roam'd along the tangled shore
    With happy hearts, and bold unfearing mien;
    Their war-songs sang they the blue waters o'er,
In all things Freedom's children, hers erelong no more.

IV.

Heard ye the eagle swooping?   Nursed in pride,

   Rome's blood-stain'd armies sought these shores, and

      flung

Her tyrant banners o'er the reckless tide:

   The waves dash'd on, but bitter chains were hung

   Round freemen's necks: a nation's heart was wrung!

Few, few, and weary, see them wending slow,

   Fair girls and hoary warriors, old and young,

To brave an exile's lot, an exile's woe,

Far from their native hearths on Cambria's wilds of snow.

V.

Then rose, as legends tell, yon turrets, piled

   By the proud victor to enchain the free;

Swiftly they rose,—but oh! when morning smiled

   First on those towers from out the golden sea,

   Where Rome's proud eagle, Britain, mock'd at thee,

Who could have guess'd the dark and wondrous story

   Of things that have been there and yet shall be?

Written too oft in letters deeply gory—

A captive's tale of tears, yet bright with deeds of glory.

VI.

Like one who bending o'er the waves that sleep
    'Mid Tyre's old fabled battlements descries
Their faint dim outline in the silent deep [1],
    Till in the shadowy light before his eyes
    Dome after dome begins ere long to rise;—
Thus the far landscape of the past we scan,
    And wondrous seem and dark its mysteries,
Till truth hath lit Time's strangely-pictured plan,
And ah! yet stranger still, the passionate heart of man.

VII.

And when I stood beside that hoary pile
    Its legends rose like phantoms of the tomb:
Spell-bound I linger'd there, and mused awhile
    On every tower and spirit-haunted room;
    Mused o'er the cells of Hope's untimely doom,

---

[1] The ruins of Tyre are said to be seen under the waves.

And the yet drearier vaulted caves below,
   Where heaven's pure light ne'er trembled through the
     gloom ;
Some with their tale of wonder, some of woe—
Here where the heart might throb, and there where tears
     might flow.

VIII.

Methought I saw two happy children lying,
   Lock'd in each other's arms, at dead of night,
Peace smiled beside, but Love stood o'er them sighing:—
   And I heard stealthy footsteps treading light—
   List!—steps of murderers?—never! for that sight
Must break a heart of marble: yet 'tis done,—
   Low smother'd groans too truly told aright
As one they lived and loved, they died as one—
None there to save them? weeping Echo answers " None."

IX.

Yet childhood is a sunny dream, and we
   Can scarcely mourn when it doth pass away.

Unclouded to heaven's sunshine; and to me

    Those towers where wingèd spirits day by day

    Have lived unmurmuring on to life's decay

Seem yet more strangely sad:—and such was thine,

    O thou whose far keen eyesight won its way

O'er Time's drear ages, till there seem'd to shine

Across the starless gulf Truth's glorious arch divine [2].

X.

Man scales the mountain-tops, but o'er the mist

    The eagle hovering seeks its native sky,

And the free clouds still wander where they list,

    And still the waves are tameless.   Thus on high

    Thy thoughts at pleasure could take wing and fly,

Though fetter'd were thy limbs, and thus didst thou

    Visit each clime and age with wandering eye,

And win a fadeless garland for thy brow,

And free with wisdom's freedom, deign to her to bow.

[2] Sir Walter Raleigh, who during his long imprisonment wrote immortal " History of the World."

XI.

A sadder turret, minstrel, bids thee linger,
  And weave a sadder strain for her that's gone [3];
O gently touch thy chords with sorrow's finger,
  Nor let thy music without tears flow on.
    Low from that tower she lean'd, while yet there shone
The rosy blush of evening in her cell;
    Her eye was raised to heaven, her look was wan,
And on her bosom tears full quickly fell,—
Sad tribute to her land, its dying child's farewell.

XII.

"Oh! other were the dreams," she weeping cried,
  "That rose and smiled upon mine infant years!
Bright were they in their freshness—all have died—
  My fancied garlands were but gemm'd with tears,
  My starry guide a meteor, and mine ears
Caught but false syren strains; yet, frail and young,
  I deem'd that star a light of other spheres,
Snatch'd at the wreath, drank in the illusive song,
And now, to-morrow ... hush! my throbs will cease ere long.

[3] Lady Jane Grey.

T

XIII.

" To-morrow—'tis a strange and fearful call—
　　To-morrow's eve and I shall be no more.
Yet why so fearful unto me ?　We all
　　Are voyaging towards a distant shore,
　　Toss'd on life's fitful billows, whose wild roar
Drowns the far music of our heavenly home:
　　A few more surging waves to traverse o'er,
Some little stormy wind, some billowy foam,
And I have gain'd my bourn—oh! ne'er again to roam."

XIV.

That morrow came; the young and lovely one
　　Was led where soon her mangled corse should lie:
There, breaking hearts and stifled sighs—and none
　　Look'd without tears on her blue tearless eye.
　　Yet seem'd she all too beautiful to die,
Ere love and gladness from her cheek had flown:—
　　Fond dreamer! knowest thou not the happy sky
Claims first the loveliest flowerets for its own ?
Heaven's nurslings, lent to earth as exiled plants alone.

XV.

I mused in sadness, for methought there fell
    Her smile on me, her loveliest, her last.   ᴠ
But hark! the watchword of the sentinel.
    Changed were my dreams—yon nightly turrets cast
    Upon my soul the image of the past;
And many were the thoughts, and wild and wide,
    Echoing of thee, my country, 'mid the blast—
There have thy monarchs fought, thy chieftains died,
And queenly hearts for thee throbb'd high with hero pride.

XVI.

Time-honour'd Towers! whence ever floated free
    Old England's banners over hearts as bold!
Within whose walls the sceptre of the sea
    Lies by the sword of mercy—where is told
    The thrilling tale o'er many a trophy old,
Where diadems rest, and helm and spear are piled,
    And standards in a thousand fights unroll'd,
Oh there the heart must lose itself, and wild
Will be its wandering-song—of vision'd dreams the child.

XVII.

I look'd upon thy walls when day was closing,
· Mighty and vast they rose upon the sight,
In massive grandeur silently reposing:
    List! 'tis the hush of evening—dimly bright
    The moon just glimmer'd, and the listless night
Was brooding over wave and tower sublime,
    When suddenly there gleam'd a fatal light
Amid those frowning ramparts—'twas the time
When all things slumber on, and nigh the midnight c

XVIII.

But hark! the crash of timbers—then the hush
    Of breathless whispering rose, and the red glow
Grew momently more vivid, and the rush
    Of hurrying footsteps echoed to and fro—
    And like a dream it pass'd of flames and woe.
I look'd upon thy walls when morn was riding
    In sunshine o'er the rosy hills, and lo!
Amid the wreck, like spectres unabiding,
Glory and Desolation hand in hand were gliding.

XIX.

The heart must catch at omens, and must weave
  From passing meteors dreams of hope or fear!
And some, my country, speak a mournful eve
  Of thy long day of glory. Far and near
  The storm-clouds, brooding round thy skirts appear;
And wailings, as of winds through woods, are heard:
  And hangs, like death, the heavy atmosphere:
And smitten as with some prophetic word
The strong foundations of the earth are moved and stirr'd.

XX.

The nations are disquieted, the heart
  Of princes ill at ease: the fearful bow
Their heads and tremble: with hush'd voice apart
  The mighty stand, with pale though dauntless brow,
  Asking of every hour—" What bringest thou ?"
And if a murmur whisper through the sky
  They hush their breath, and cry, " It cometh now."
What cometh ? Stay—it heeds thee not to fly,
Unknown, though on its way—unseen, yet surely nigh.

XXI.

But who shall dare, though storms are round thy way,
  To write upon thy banners, Ichabod [4] ?
Thy strength is not in ramparts built of clay,
  Nor in thy fearless children, who have trod
  The waves as proudly as their native sod ;
But heavenly watchers aye have guarded thee—
  God is thy refuge, and thy rampart God.
Here lies thy might, His arm thy trust shall be
Amid the wildest storms of Time's untravell'd sea.

[4] " The glory is departed."

Trinity College, 1844.

CAUBUL.

. . . . 'Επεὶ οὔτι μοι αἴτιοί εισιν
οὐ γὰρ πώποτ' ἐμὰς βοῦς ἤλασαν, οὐδὲ μεν ἵππους,
οὐδέ ποτ' ἐν Φθίῃ ἐριβώλακι, βωτιανείρῃ,
καρπὸν ἐδηλήσαντ'. ἐπειὴ μάλα πολλὰ μεταξὺ
οὔρεά τε σκιόεντα θάλασσά τε ἠχήεσσα.—ILIAD, i. 153.

I.

" Sweep o'er thy strings, and hymn the gorgeous East,
  Clime of the sun, and of the roseate morning."
Dim voices whisper'd thus my soul, and ceased.
  And straightway at the echo of their warning
  Came visions many a one in bright adorning,
Clustering like clouds instinct with light around me :
  And music, as of winds and waters, scorning
The slumber of the twilight hills, spell-bound me,
Till where the stars had left the dew-bright sunshine found
    me.

II.

Oh land of dreams and legendary song,
 Strange are the wonders they of fabling story
Tell of thy haunted scenery ! Far along
 The maze of thousand years through gloom and glor
 Like some wild landscape wrapt in vapours hoary,
The eye must wander, ere it reach the time,
 Ye Eastern shores, where mystery hung not o'er ye :
Dim forms sweep looming through the mists of crime,
Or stand in light apparell'd on those hills sublime.

III.

And ever as I pondered, empires vast
 Rose on my view, and vanish'd as they came ;
And heroes meteor-like before me pass'd,
 Their pathway dimm'd with blood and track'd by flam
 Yet fell they all in darkness. Haply Fame
Shed transient tears for them ; but soon there shone
 Another star far flashing—and the same
Brief tale was told—and ever and anon
Though gleaming high as heaven, I look'd, and they we
 gone.

IV.

But one[1] there was, whose dazzling train of fire
    Startled the sleeping night in her repose;
The blue heavens kindled as he pass'd—the choir
    Of stars was troubled. From afar he rose,
    Where in the evening light there faintly glows
Mild radiance o'er the hills of Macedon;
    And rushing forth, despite a nation's throes,
Through blood and breaking hearts and sorrows wan,
To Persia's confines drove his stormy chariot on.

V.

[2]Thy rugged passes, Caubul, saw that host,
    As with glad banners to the breezes flung,
Slow winding, o'er thy mountain range it cross'd:
    And thy wild air heard victor pæans sung,
    And strange sweet accents of entrancing tongue.

---

[1] Alexander the Great.

[2] " From this point (Herât), starting in the end of October, Alexander marched to the Kabool valley, through a country occupied by Indians, and bordering on Arachotia."—PRINSEP'S *Affghanistan*.

He linger'd not: the far-off fabulous sea
   He saw, and smiled : but Fate above him hung :
He fetter'd all the earth, yet was not free:
All nations bow'd to him—he bow'd, O Death, to thee.

VI.

And ages pass'd away like dreams: till soon
   A victor footstep trod those hills once more.
'Twas night; and lit up by the silver moon,
    As streams a torrent from the hills, stream'd o'er
   Wild children of the barren Scythian shore.
Ah ! woe for those who on the vine-clad plain
   Sleep on unconscious as they slept of yore!
Death wakes ; and echoing to the skies amain
Is heard the shout of nations—" Hail, great Tamerlane ! "

VII.

Yes! such have been the tempests that have pass'd,
   Ye Affghan heights, across your crests of snow,
Or like the rushing of the nightly blast
   Swept by in wildness and in wrath below;

Yet there unchanged amid the troubled flow
Of time's wild waters, silently ye rise,
 And reckless of the whirlwind march of woe,
With that strange spirit-voice that in ye lies
Hold mystic communings with yonder starry skies.

VIII.

[3]Perchance ye are whispering how in Caubul's vale,
 Erst bloom'd the flowers of Eden pure and wild,
How waters gush'd from springs that could not fail,
 And earth, in one bright infant dream beguiled,
 Beneath the smile of heaven look'd up and smiled.
Oh, why o'er time's dear ocean rise to view
 The monuments in crime and bloodshed piled?
Why seem the waters with oblivious dew
Too oft to hide from sight the beautiful and true?

[3] " Hindoo and Persian traditions go so far as to state that the
progenitors of mankind lived in that mountainous tract which extends
from Bulkh and Affghanistan to the Ganges. . . . And the river Pison of
Scripture is said to compass the whole country of Havilah, and Havilah
is supposed to be Caubul."—ATKINSON'S *Preface.*

IX.

The curtains of the past are round me closing;
    I may not lift them more: all silently
Behind its vaporous folds, in death reposing,
    The bygone ages slumber. But for me
    An island, loveliest of the deep-blue sea,
In beauty smiles far o'er the ocean foam:
    Mine heart goes out towards that fair countree,
Thoughts o'er a thousand long-loved landscapes roam,
A thousand spots are dear . . . . it is my island-home.

X.

And can it be her wondrous destinies
    With yours, ye Eastern regions, are inwove?
Lo! cradled in the storms, and under skies
    Cloud-robed and starless ever forced to rove,
    Her infant empire with the tempests strove:—
Heaven had not will'd its shipwreck—for the shroud
    Of Superstition o'er that land above
Hung shadowing; so the East in silence bow'd,
And Britain's banners waved triumphant through the clo

XI.

'Chill sweeps the night-blast o'er the Affghan hills:
  No eye that sleeps in Caubul's walls to-night!
None talked of home: a strange foreboding fills
    The hearts of all, and many an anxious sight
    Looks forth upon the darkness, where the bright
Far-flickering watch-fires blazed; some trembling lay
    All night within around the camp-fire's light,
Some on the rampart wait in dark dismay
The morrow's blood-stain'd march—the awful break of day.

XII.

The mother look'd upon her babe, and sobb'd;
    The husband clasp'd his wife, his breast was torn
With anguish, and with grief past utterance throbb'd,—
    He knew what horrors *she* must pass at morn;
    Youth wept there, with her sister Beauty, born

---

¹ The night before the British troops left Caubul on their retreat has been selected.

Like her for sunshine, now like her in gloom;
  And innocent childhood, as in playful scorn,
Smiled on them both, but all its rosy bloom
Chased not from heavy hearts the morrow and the tomb.

XIII.

Slowly morn flush'd the mountains.   Hurriedly
  The mingled host of women, children, men,
Those ramparts left, and left them but to die.
  Oh! bear the gentle gently.   Hark! again
  The war-cry of the treacherous foe—and then
Death in its countless forms beset their road,
  Till corses throng'd each deep and rocky glen;
And where the wilds of snow with slaughter glow'd,
All crimson'd on its path the icy torrent flow'd.

XIV.

'Twas scenery, too, where Horror sat sublime:
  The bleak hills rose precipitous to heaven;
And up their snow-clad sides the mists did climb,
  Sole wanderers there, and by the wild winds driven
  Hover'd like spectres; through the rocks were rive

Dark chasms, that echo'd to the torrent's voice,
　Where never pierced the stars of morn or even;
No life, no light the wanderer to rejoice,
But gloom, and doubt, and death, the region of their choice.

XV.

And through these gorges, that in darkness frown'd
　When o'er them stretch'd the deep-blue summer-sky,
'Mid snows and wintry storms their pathway wound,
　The dying and the dead—and none pass'd by
　To fold their mantle or to close their eye.
Foes lurk'd by every secret cleft and cave,
　And to their fire the sharp rocks made reply—
One short stern death-knell o'er the fallen brave
There in that awful pass, their battle-field and grave.

XVI.

And deeds were done of pure and high devotion,
　Deeds of heroic fame—but where are they
To tell their story?—like the gloomy ocean
　Strewn with the wrecks of nations, far away
　On stranger hills their mouldering corses lay;

One only struggled through, exhausted, pale,
    The sole survivor of that proud array,
And death and fear, at his most ghastly tale,
Cast slowly over all their shadowy silent veil.

XVII.

Chains for the brave, and solitude and sorrow!
    Ay, prison-hours for gentler beings too!
Oh! they were faint for freedom, and the morrow
    Never seem'd dawning on their night of woe:
    Young hearts were there, and tears would sometimes
        flow,   .
When faëry home-scenes crowded on their view,
    Clad in unearthly beauty, for the glow
Of love still seem'd to light up all anew,
And faith that leant on God in suffering proved most true.

XVIII.

Love[b] is a lamp on tossing billows cast,
    Yet many waters cannot quench its flame;

---

[b] "Many waters cannot quench love, neither can the floods drown
it."—*Solomon's Song*, viii. 7.

Love is a bark adrift before the blast,
  Which still rides struggling on through taunts or fame,
  Amid the floods unchanging and the same; ·
For love hath music, music of its own,
  (Though none have whisper'd whence those harpings
      came,)
Which vibrates with a strange mysterious tone
pon the ear of him who weepeth all alone. ·

XIX.

On, brothers, to the rescue!   See, they come
  With floating pennons and undaunted pride,
And victor-shouts and roll of martial drum!
  Alas! within those defiles scatter'd wide
  Their brethren's whitening bones are now their guide:
Woe for the sod beneath their chargers' feet!
  For Spring with trembling hand hath drawn aside
(Wont to disclose a thousand flowerets sweet)
he fearful veil of death! a shroud! a winding-sheet!

XX.

Their camp-fires, in the dark of night's repose,
  Far glimmering in the pass below did gleam

U

Like the stars burning o'er them, till to those

　　Lone watchers on the mountains war might seem

　　But the dim splendours of a phantom dream.

On, brothers, on! nor pause, nor rest, nor sleep

　　By cavern, pine, or rock, or torrent-stream,

Nor linger o'er your comrades' bones and weep,

Till victors yet once more through Caubul's gates ye sweep!

XXI.

And what of those who pined in gloom the while?

　　No victor armies their deliverers were;

But God, who heard from their far native isle

　　The mourner's sobbings, and the sabbath prayer[6]

Flow for the captive and the prisoner,

　　Threw open wide their prison-gates[7]; and she

　　Who, angel-like, stoop weeping by them there,

---

[6] *The Sabbath prayer:* "That it may please Thee to preserve all that travel by land or by water . . . *and to show Thy pity upon all prisoners and captives.*"—*The Litany.*

[7] "Fortunately discontent prevailed among the soldiers of our guard, and their commandant began to intrigue with Major Pottinger for our release. A large reward was held out to him, and he swallowed the bait. The Huzarah chiefs were gained over, and we commenced our return towards Cabul."—EYRE, p. 316.

Immortal Love, sprang o'er the billowy sea,
And stole into our homes, and whisper'd, "They are free."

XXII.

What if dim visions of the future throng
 Around my soul, and voices from afar
Tell that those blood-stain'd mountains shall ere long
 See England's armies, Russia's brazen car [s],
 Roll o'er them for a sterner deadlier war?—
The dark night lowering darkest, ere the sky
 Catch the strange beauty of the Morning-star?—
The lion and the eagle's struggling cry,
Wrapt in the mountain-storm, while lightnings hurtle by?—

XXIII.

Enough, enough—for now the fitful roar
 Of strife grows fainter, till its echo dies
Within me, and my heart is sad no more.
 See! landscapes brighter yet than Eastern skies

[s] "The two great powers which have now in an indelible manner imprinted their image upon the human species, England and Russia, are there (speaking of the East) slowly but inevitably coming into collision."— ALISON's *French Revol.*, vol. viii. chap. 64.

Dawn in far prospect on my tearful eyes,
And from on high come trembling through my soul
Waves of sphere-music, dream-like melodies,
Chasing life's myriad discords: earth's control
Is passing from me now: celestial scenes unroll.

XXIV.

Yes! o'er those wilds shall flow pure crystal fountains—
Fountains of life divine, and love and light:
How beautiful upon thy morning mountains
Stand messengers of peace!   The shades of night
Are passing, and disclose on every height
The standard of the Cross; for God hath spoken,
And gleaming through the storm-clouds softly bright,
Far o'er the hills, in beauty all unbroken
The Gospel rainbow writes its own transparent token.

Trinity College, 1845.

CÆSAR'S INVASION OF BRITAIN.

"His ego nec metas rerum, nec tempora pono :
Imperium sine fine dedi."

HAIL, solitary Rome: amid the tombs
Of ages, and the monuments that lie
Strewn far o'er the wild howling waste of time,
Thyself by cloud and tempest not unscathed,
Thou risest proudly eminent: of gods
And godlike heroes thou the haunt and home:
Nurse thou of kingliest spirits: who vouchsafed
Few words but deathless deeds; who scoff'd to write
Their records on the perishable scrolls
Of man, fast fading, likest to the beams
The sun imprints upon the transient clouds
Of evening; but with conquest's iron pen,
The world their tablet, carved that history out

On Eastern coasts and Western, South and North,

On trackless seas, and lands long lost in night,

On wrecks of empires and on hearts of men.

Strange, awful characters! which dark decay

Hath not as yet effaced, nor chance, nor change,

Nor storm, nor ruin, nor the tide of years,

Though ever chafing o'er them.   Ne'er before

Saw earth such gloomy strength, nor ever since

Its like hath witness'd:—the last awful form

[1] Of human might, in dimmest lineaments

By God foreshadow'd: warriors they, who reck'd

Of nothing, or of God or man, save strength.

And they were strong, strong-hearted, strong in arms.

Earth stood astonied at the sight.   No lapse,

No break, no faltering in the dreadful march

Of those stern iron conquerors.   On they strode,

Like men of fate, trampling beneath their feet

All other names, all other destinies,

---

[1] "After this I saw in the night visions, and behold a fourth beast, dreadful and terrible, and strong exceedingly; and it had great iron teeth: it devoured and brake in pieces, and stamped the residue with the feet of it."—Dan. vii. 7.

Like dust before them.   Throned on her seven hills

Rome, inaccessible herself, beheld

Her sons go forth to battle, and her glory

Quenching all meaner lights, and scattering far

The darkness of unnumber'd years: as when

The sun, at his Almighty Maker's word,

First in the everlasting vault of heaven

Hung pendulous, and from before him drove

The waves of Chaos, and tempestuous night,

Rolling in billowy surges ever back,

Back to their own abysmal shoreless void,

From his celestial presence.   Time roll'd on,

And still with time thy glory brighten'd, still

Thine empire grew with time.   The nations saw,

And trembled; and the silence of thy might

Seem'd to their ears oppressive eloquence

That none might interrupt: when thou didst speak,

Thy voice of thunder shook the startled world,

With lightning gleams of steel accompanied,

And flashes of swift vengeance.   Awfully

Peace brooded once more over weary lands,

And weary hearts too smiled.   But round thy skirts,

Clinging like night, dark masses of dark clouds
Hung yet, and mantled in their giant folds
The vast Unknown beyond, though voices thence
Came sometime, dimly muttering wars and woe.

   Such was the gloom that hung around thy shores,
Albion, and shrouded from the spoiler's eye
Thy forests, and far mountains, and green vales,
And rocky fells, and rivers fleet and free:—
They knew thee not how beautiful: when known,
Dark desolation, like a haggard dream,
Stole o'er the sunshine of thy countenance,
And scared thy smiles, and left thee pale and wan,
A widow and a captive. Ah, not thus
Whilom thy children chased their forest prey,
Or roam'd the morning hills, by streams that spake
Of light and freedom, to the fetterless winds
Responsive: or at eventide not thus
Were wont to linger on thy cliffs, where last
The golden sunshine slumber'd, till the stars
Came forth, upon their vigils dawning: bright
They seem'd as spirit-eyes and pure, wherewith

Thy Druid bards enlink'd all earthly things
Aforetime, by wild legendary lore:
Not thus the reckless warrior grasp'd his spear,
Or freeman spake to freeman.   But when thou
Didst tremble, it was not beneath the eye
Of tyrant man; but at those awful powers,
Who ever, as thy fabling prophets sung,
Dwelt, mystery-clad, in mountain, vale, or cloud,
Or ocean pathway, tabernacling there
As in meet home, whose voices might be heard,
Whose foot-prints traced by wrecks o'er sea and land,
What time the thunders roll'd, or lightnings gleam'd.

    Those mystic days were number'd.   There was one
Who long had trodden on the earth, as treads .
The eagle on the gory plain it spurns,
Whose kingly heart was gasping for great deeds,
Deeds that his right hand taught him, and whose eye
Drank from the nightly stars heroic thoughts,
And dreams of high achievement.   Warrior king!
Thy mother city knew thee when a child,
And proudly knew thee, nursing up thy soul

For glory: the snow-crested Apennines,
The Alps far mingling with the clouds and skies,
With their clear glaciers gleaming to the moon,
Knew thee: Germania's forests knew thee: Gaul,
Vine-clad, and water'd by a thousand streams,
Maugre her fierce defenders, knew thee well,
Great Cæsar, weeping that she could not find
Thy peer: and now upon her vanquish'd shores
Deep musing, having march'd with lion springs
From conquest on to conquest, thou dost cast
Long glances o'er the twilight ocean waves
Upon that land of mystery, that lies
Far in the blue horizon dimly seen.

Some talk'd of merchandise, and pearls, and wealth;
Of trophies and of triumphs some; and some
Of battle spoils and blue-eyed maidens fair
To grace their homes far-distant, thoughts whereof
Clung to their rugged hearts; a new strange world,
Some whisper'd, lay before their path, whose sky
At dead of night was flush'd with gorgeous flames
And rushing meteors, and whose only bound

Was everlasting ice;—enough for thee,
It knew not Rome's eternal name or thine;
And it shall know them straightway, though it learn
Mid dying throes, and though thou teach thyself.

Morn's silver twilight hung above the waves:
Seaward the gales blew freshly: far aloft
Clouds swiftly track'd the sky: one single star
Still linger'd in the dawning east, as if
To steal a glance at day, but soon withdrew;
The lordly sun came forth; and all was life
And in the harbour tumult: crowded there
Twice forty gallant ships, and on their decks
Brave hearts, that burn'd to vie with Britain's sons
In battle.　Over them their streamers waved
That way themselves would go; nor long they paused
Expectant: thrice the brazen trumpet blown,
Each galley loosed her moorings: one by one
Stately they weigh'd beneath the freshening wind,
And the free waters bare them swiftly on
To sound of martial notes, and aching eyes
Gazed after that brave fleet the livelong day.

And deem ye that an easy booty lies
Before your bloodless arms? or they that throng
Their isle's rock-ramparts, think ye they have come
With open arms to greet ye?   But their chief,
First on the foremost galley, saw their ranks,
Death boding, and beheld the white cliffs crown'd
With   shields   and   bristling   spears,   and   steeds   of
        war,
And chariots numberless.   Along the coast
Swiftly they sail'd, if haply crags less stern
Might yield them fairer landing, swift the while
The Britons streaming o'er the rocks and hills
Kept pace beside, and vaunted death should greet
The tyrant and his legions, ere their foot
Polluted freedom's soil.   Then rose the din
Of battle: in the waves midway they met
Rome's proudest warriors, and the foaming surge
Dash'd crimson-dyed: and scythe-arm'd chariots swept
The shore in unresisted might, and darts·
Fell ever in swift tempest: once again
In proud derision Britain shook her spear,
And bade them take, an if it liked them well,

Such iron welcome to her freeborn hills[2].

And Rome a moment quail'd; but[3] one who grasp'd

An eagle in his left hand, in his right

A sword, cried, " Romans, down into the waves:

" On! or betray our eagle to the foe;

" I'll on for Rome and Cæsar!"   Scarce he spoke,

And from the prow leapt fearless, and straightway

His comrades round him throng'd, and the fierce fight

Grew fiercer 'mid the angry tide: but still

The star of Rome rode prevalent in heaven,

And Britain's sons, borne backward by the host

Of spears, and gnashing with remorse and pride,

Fell from that iron phalanx; and Rome's chief

Stood conqueror on Britannia's beetling cliffs.

Not thus shall Albion yield thee her fair fields,

Great Julius, and not thus beneath thy rod

Affrighted bow and tremble; nor is hers

---

[2] See Macaulay's " Lays of Rome," Horatius, stan. xlvii.

[3] "Atque nostris militibus cunctantibus ... qui x. legionis aquilam
rebat ... 'Desilite,' inquit, ' milites, nisi vultis aquilam hostibus
rodere; ego certe meum Reipublicæ et Imperatori officium præstitero.'"
-CÆSAR, *de Bell. Gall.*, liber iv.   Cf. hic et passim.

The arena thou must tread to bind the crown
Around thy warrior temples, and ascend
Thine envious throne: a few brief hours, and lo!
Heaven's tempests, wild and baleful, thy frail fleet
Have shatter'd, and in haste across the sea
Thine armies seek repose. What though ere long
With happier omen, and with prouder host,
The subject waters bare thee hitherwards
Once more?   What though, through battle and throug
    storm,
And rivers running blood, and harvest fields
Stain'd with the gore of thousands, thou didst press
On to the heart of Britain? what if there
Her chieftains bow'd a moment to thy rod,
And freedom taught their free hearts slavish ways?
'Twas but a moment: Heaven had other deeds
For thee to do, and other destinies
Loom'd dimly on the future's clouded skirts
Before thine eagle eye.   Nor didst thou prove
A recreant.   Fare thee, kingly warrior, well.
Go grasp thy regal sceptre, go ascend
Thy world-wide throne! to other hands than thine,

And years yet labouring in the future's womb,

'Tis given to bow beneath a Roman yoke

Free Albion's neck, and lead her captive kings

In fetters, and pollute her smiling homes

With foulest wrong and insult: bitterness

All hearts possessing: till her warrior chiefs

Weep tears of blood, her maidens tears of shame,

And Britain writhes beneath the iron scourge

Of conquest.

       So in after days there rush'd

Rude whirlwind storms of war and death and woe

O'er that fair isle, and shatter'd into dust

The blood-built fabrics of an idol faith,

Whereat dark centuries had labour'd: soon

They fell before those fierce avenging storms,

Yet storms, that in their dark and gloomy folds

Bare germs of happier days, and dawning lights

Of love and mercy; as the lightning-gleams

Course not along the star-paved vault of heaven,

But from the earth-born thunder-clouds flash forth

In beauty and resplendence.   Soon from thee,

My native isle, their stern behest fulfill'd

The clouds of wrath and tempest roll'd away

Dream-like; and following on their wasted track

Pure healing sunshine, bountiful in good,

Stole o'er thy sorrowing landscapes; and ere long

A Christian Church on Albion's shores arose,

And pointed to the skies, and call'd the stars

To witness, that in tempest, as in calm,

Heaven works its own eternal destiny.

Trinity College, 1846.

YESTERDAY, TO-DAY, AND FOR EVER:

A Poem in Twelve Books.

By EDWARD HENRY BICKERSTETH, M.A.,

VICAR OF CHRIST CHURCH, HAMPSTEAD, AND CHAPLAIN TO THE
BISHOP OF RIPON.

CONTENTS.

RIVINGTONS,

LONDON, OXFORD, AND CAMBRIDGE.

OPINIONS OF THE PRESS.

"We feel assured that the reader will feel grateful to us for having made him acquainted with the most simple, the richest, and the most perfect sacred poem which recent days have produced."—*Morning Advertiser.*

"This is a remarkable poem, and one likely to attract a great deal of attention. While antique in form, it is modern in spirit, and is animated by an enthusiasm which carries the reader along without any sense of weariness. . . . . As a poetical vision the picture of the intermediate state is perfect."—*The Imperial Review.*

"The epic narrative begins with an account of the creation of angels and men: here he treads the same ground as Milton, treating the subject differently and with great power. . . . . The last four books are to our mind the best. Their subjects are more untrodden, and they are full of bold imagination. As materialized theology in its most poetical form, we must give them the highest praise. . . . . It is a poem worth reading, worthy of attentive study; full of noble thoughts, beautiful diction, and high imagination; and, more than all, penetrated with a spirit of holiness which cannot fail to purify and sanctify the mind of the reader."—*The Standard.*

" We venture to predict for this poem a considerable amount of popularity. . . . . Without for a moment instituting any comparison, we may remark that Pollok's 'Course of Time' rose before us as we ran over the pages, and saw the scope and design of the book. But it is more sustained, and far more sober and regular than that once popular production, and it has far higher literary claims."—*Clerical Journal.*

" If any poem is destined to endure in the companionship of Milton's hitherto matchless epic, we believe it will be '*Yesterday, To-day, and For Ever*'."—*The Globe.*

" He writes like a man who cultivates at once reverence and earnestness of thought, who does not despise the aids of learning or forget the limitations of our nature, who possesses considerable imitative grace, and has in his composition a large element of affectionate tenderness."—*The Guardian.*

" Mr. Bickersteth's work is not a crude effusion. He tells us that it has been elaborated in his mind through many years; and we will say that his labour has not been in vain. He has produced a poem which we believe will be largely read, which will dwell in the memory of those who read it, and which will leave often, we doubt not, holy thoughts in the hearts of those who have followed him from the deathbed of weakness on to the endless life of power in the joyful mansions of our Father's house."—*Christian Observer.*

" In these light-miscellany days, there is a spiritual refreshment in the spectacle of a man girding up the loins of his mind to the task of producing a genuine epic. And it is true poetry. There is a definiteness, a crispness about it, which in these moist, viewy, hazy days, is no less invigorating than novel."—*Daily Review, Edinburgh.*

" But even where this is the case, Mr. Bickersteth's verse has about it a freshness and a charm which save it from mediocrity, and will ensure for it readers and admirers. . . . . The whole first book, 'The Seer's death and descent into Hades,' is really of high merit. . . . . The same strain of felicitous description prevails in the second book, 'The Paradise of the Blessed Dead.' The descriptions of the Seer's meeting with his lost babes and with the glorified from among his own flock are very beautiful."—*The Contemporary Review.*

"It is impossible to read these lines (Book ii. 155—202), so full of power, and yet so exquisite in their tenderness, without finding one's self strangely moved, the spiritual pulse quickened, and the heart glowing with fresher love to Christ."—*The Presbyterian, Philadelphia.*

"This remarkable work may do as much towards fashioning our theology as 'Paradise Lost,' probably more."—*Zion's Herald, Boston.*

"These three visions are, indeed, but different views of the same grand objects of human thought and interest—sin, redemption, and salvation. But, as Milton, because he wrote out of the depths of his own intellect and heart, and from the inspiration of his own genius, neither copied nor imitated Dante, so Bickersteth has shown himself a great and original poet, by treating substantially the same themes as Milton, without the least appearance of treading in his steps, and in a style singularly original and fresh. He has conceived his subject for himself, has handled it after a fashion of his own; and, while embodying in it the type of religious thought and feeling which belongs distinctively to his time, has impressed on the whole work his own intellectual and moral image as completely as either of his illustrious predecessors did on his.

"Beginning with the death of the Seer, and his entrance into Paradise, the poem recounts the whole drama of earth's moral history, in the form of a narrative from the lips of Oriel, his guardian angel. Our limits will not allow us to go into any analysis of the action represented. We can only say that it exhibits a rich and creative imagination, an exquisite purity of taste, and a power of delineation that leaves little to be desired. In a poem of such length, here and there a feeble line or a questionable expression must almost necessarily occur. But nothing is vague and half-conceived, or indistinctly told. The language is simple and precise, rarely turgid, or strained, or marred with affectations of any sort. In the mode of conceiving and describing the scenery and life of the invisible world, there is a felicitous medium between the grossness of sheer materialism on the one hand, and the shadowy tenuity of an unreal spiritualism on the other. Aside from the brief and simple statements of the Scriptures themselves, we have read nothing, to our thought, at all comparable to these pictures of the intermediate state of departed souls. In the progress of the dramatic development of the plan, the interest is well sustained, and holds the unflagging attention of the reader to the last.

"If, along with a power to appreciate the charming language and the harmonies of verse, one has also a heart warm with devout affection and in quick sympathy with what is truly spiritual and divine, he cannot but find pleasure, absorbing and intense, yet altogether healthful, in this noble contribution to English sacred literature. No Christian heart, it would seem, can fail to be refreshed and made permanently better by finding itself borne up, as on mighty wings, into the highest regions of religious thought, and enabled to study, in one comprehensive view, the great scheme of eternal Providence for the recovery of the human race to holiness and life. We have felt, on laying down this volume, as if we had been for some time wandering through the bewildering loveliness of Paradise, breathing its vital air, communing with angels and the spirits of the just made perfect, and beholding the face and hearing the voice of the Blessed One whom the holy in all worlds adore. Such, we can hardly doubt, will be the experience of many who will read and re-read its quickening and inspiring pages."—*From a Review by the Rev. Ray Palmer, D.D., New York.*

GILBERT AND RIVINGTON, PRINTERS, ST. JOHN'S SQUARE, LONDON.

New Works

IN COURSE OF PUBLICATION BY

Messrs. RIVINGTON,

WATERLOO PLACE, LONDON;

HIGH STREET, OXFORD; TRINITY STREET, CAMBRIDGE.

November, 1870.

DICTIONARY OF DOCTRINAL AND HISTORICAL THEOLOGY.

By Various Writers.

Edited by the Rev. John Henry Blunt, M.A., F.S.A., Editor of 'The Annotated Book of Common Prayer.'

One vol., imperial 8vo. 42*s.*

The Principles of the CATHEDRAL SYSTEM
VINDICATED and FORCED upon MEMBERS of CATHEDRAL FOUNDATIONS.

Eight Sermons, preached in the Cathedral Church of the Holy and Undivided Trinity of Norwich.

By **Edward Meyrick Goulburn**, D.D., Dean of Norwich, late Prebendary of St. Paul's, and one of Her Majesty's Chaplains.

Crown 8vo. 5*s.*

LONDON, OXFORD, & CAMBRIDGE.

I

ELEMENTS OF RELIGION.

Lectures delivered at St. James's, Piccadilly, in Lent, 1870.
By **Henry Parry Liddon**, D.C.L., Canon of St. Paul's, and
Ireland Professor of Exegesis in the University of Oxford.

Crown 8vo. [*In the Press.*

A MANUAL OF LOGIC;

Or, a Statement and Explanation of the Laws of Formal Thought.
By **Henry J. Turrell**, M.A., Oxon.

Square crown 8vo. 2s. 6d.

THE PSALMS translated from the HEBREW.

With Notes, chiefly Exegetical.
By **William Kay**, D.D., Rector of Great Leighs; late Principal of
Bishop's College, Calcutta.

8vo. [*In the Press.*

SERMONS.

By **Henry Melvill**, B.D., Canon of St. Paul's, and Chaplain
in Ordinary to the Queen.

New Edition. Two vols. Crown 8vo. 5s. each.

THE ORIGIN AND DEVELOPMENT OF RELIGIOUS BELIEF.

By **S. Baring-Gould**, M.A., Author of 'Curious Myths of the
Middle Ages.'

PART II. CHRISTIANITY. *8vo.* 15s.
PART I. HEATHENISM AND MOSAISM. *8vo.* 15s.

PARISH MUSINGS; or, DEVOTIONAL POEMS.

By **John S. B. Monsell**, LL.D., Rural Dean, and Rector of
St. Nicholas Guildford.

New Edition. 18mo. Limp cloth, 1s. 6d.; or in cover, 1s.

LONDON, OXFORD, & CAMBRIDGE.

2

THE WITNESS of ST. JOHN to CHRIST;

Being the Boyle Lectures for 1870.

With an Appendix on the Authorship and Integrity of St. John's Gospel and the Unity of the Johannine Writings.

By the Rev. Stanley Leathes, M.A., Minister of St. Philip's, Regent Street, and Professor of Hebrew, King's College, London.

8vo. 10s. 6d.

THE ELEGIES OF PROPERTIUS,

Translated into English Verse.

By Charles Robert Moore, M.A., late Scholar of Corpus Christi College, Oxford.

Small 8vo. [*In the Press.*

'THE ATHANASIAN CREED,'

And its Usage in the English Church: an Investigation as to the Original Object of the Creed and the Growth of prevailing Misconceptions regarding it.

A Letter to the Very Reverend W. F. Hook, D.D., F.R.S., Dean of Chichester, from C. A. Swainson, D.D., Canon of the Cathedral, and Examining Chaplain to the Lord Bishop of Chichester; Norrisian Professor of Divinity, Cambridge.

Crown 8vo. 3s. 6d.

PRAYERS AND MEDITATIONS FOR THE HOLY COMMUNION.

With a Preface by C. J. Ellicott, D.D., Lord Bishop of Gloucester and Bristol.

With Rubrics in red. Royal 32mo. 2s. 6d.

THE SHEPHERD OF HERMAS.

Translated into English, with an Introduction and Notes.

By Charles H. Hoole, M.A., Senior Student of Christ Church, Oxford.

Fcap. 8vo. 4s. 6d.

LONDON, OXFORD, & CAMBRIDGE.

3

MATERIALS AND MODELS FOR GREEK
AND LATIN PROSE COMPOSITION.

Selected and Arranged by **J. Y. Sargent**, M.A. Tutor, late Fellow of
Magdalen College, Oxford; and **T. F. Dallin**, M.A., Fellow
and Tutor of Queen's College, Oxford.

Crown 8vo. 7s. 6d.

THE STAR OF CHILDHOOD.

A First Book of Prayers and Instruction for Children.

Compiled by a Priest.

Edited by the Rev. **T. T. Carter**, M.A., Rector of Clewer, Berks.

With Illustrations. *Royal 16mo.* 2s. 6d.

THE DOCTRINE of RECONCILIATION TO
GOD BY JESUS CHRIST.

Seven Lectures, preached during Lent, 1870, with a Prefatory Essay.

By **W. H. Fremantle**, M.A., Rector of St. Mary's, Bryanston Square.

Fcap. 8vo. 2s.

PROGRESSIVE EXERCISES IN LATIN
ELEGIAC VERSE.

By **C. G. Gepp**, B.A., late Junior Student of Christ Church, Oxford,
and Assistant Master at Tonbridge School.

Small 8vo. [*In the Press.*

SELF-RENUNCIATION.

From the French. With Introduction by the Rev. **T. T. Carter**,
M.A., Rector of Clewer.

Crown 8vo. [*In the Press.*

LONDON, OXFORD, & CAMBRIDGE.

THE HIDDEN LIFE OF THE SOUL.

From the French. By the Author of 'A Dominican Artist,' 'Life of Madame Louise de France,' etc., etc.
Crown 8vo.   5s.

ANCIENT HYMNS

From the Roman Breviary. For Domestic Use every Morning and Evening of the Week, and on the Holy Days of the Church.

To which are added, Original Hymns, principally of Commemoration and Thanksgiving for Christ's Holy Ordinances.

By **Richard Mant**, D.D., sometime Lord Bishop of Down and Connor.

New Edition. Small 8vo. 5s.   *[Nearly ready.*

The First Six Books of HOMER'S ODYSSEY.

Edited for the use of Schools, with an Introduction and English Notes by **Henry Musgrave Wilkins**, M.A., Fellow of Merton College, Oxford.

Crown 8vo.   *[In preparation.*

A HISTORY of the Holy EASTERN CHURCH.

The Patriarchate of Antioch, to the Middle of the Fifth Century.

By the Rev. **John Mason Neale**, D.D., late Warden of Sackville College, East Grinsted.

Followed by a History of the Patriarchs of Antioch, translated from the Greek of Constantius I., Patriarch of Constantinople.

Edited, with an Introduction, by **George Williams**, B.D., Vicar of Ringwood, late Fellow of King's College, Cambridge.

8vo.   *[In the Press.*

ESSAYS ON THE PLATONIC ETHICS.

By **Thomas Maguire**, LL.D. ex S.T.C.D., Professor of Latin, Queen's College, Galway.

8vo. 5s.

LONDON, OXFORD, & CAMBRIDGE.

5

ST. JOHN CHRYSOSTOM'S LITURGY.

Translated by **H. C. Romanoff**, Author of 'Sketches of the Rites and Customs of the Greco-Russian Church.'

With Illustrations. Square crown 8vo. [*In the Press.*

THE SAYINGS OF THE GREAT FORTY DAYS,

Between the Resurrection and Ascension, regarded as the Outlines of the Kingdom of God. In Five Discourses. With an Examination of Dr. Newman's Theory of Developments.

By **George Moberly**, D.C.L., Bishop of Salisbury.

Fourth Edition. Uniform with Brighstone Sermons.

Crown 8vo. [*In the Press.*

DEMOSTHENIS ORATIONES PUBLICAE.

Edited by **G. H. Heslop**, M.A., late Fellow and Assistant Tutor of Queen's College, Oxford; Head Master of St. Bees.

Part III. De Falsâ Legatione. Forming a new Part of 'Catena Classicorum.'

Crown 8vo. [*In the Press.*

DEMOSTHENIS ORATIONES PRIVATAE.

Edited by the Rev. **Arthur Holmes**, M.A., Fellow and Lecturer of Clare College, Cambridge; Lecturer and late Fellow of St. John's College,

Part I. De Coronâ. Forming a new Part of 'Catena Classicorum,'

Crown 8vo. [*In the Press.*

THE LIFE OF JUSTIFICATION.

A Series of Lectures delivered in Substance at All Saints', Margaret Street, in Lent, 1870.

By the Rev. **George Body**, B.A., Rector of Kirkby Misperton.

Crown 8vo. [*In the Press.*

LONDON, OXFORD, & CAMBRIDGE.

6

THE ILIAD OF HOMER.

Translated by **J. G. Cordery**, late of Balliol College, Oxford, and now of H. M. Bengal Civil Service.

Two vols. 8vo.

DICTIONARY OF SECTS, HERESIES, AND SCHOOLS OF THOUGHT.

By Various Writers.

Edited by the Rev. **John Henry Blunt**, M.A., F.S.A.; Editor of 'The Annotated Book of Common Prayer.'

(FORMING THE SECOND PORTION OF THE 'SUMMARY OF THEOLOGY AND ECCLESIASTICAL HISTORY,' WHICH MESSRS. RIVINGTON HAVE IN COURSE OF PREPARATION AS A 'THESAURUS THEOLOGICUS' FOR THE CLERGY AND LAITY OF THE CHURCH OF ENGLAND.)

Imperial 8vo.   [*In preparation.*

A PLAIN ACCOUNT OF THE ENGLISH BIBLE,

From the Earliest Times of its Translation to the Present Day.

By **John Henry Blunt**, M.A., Vicar of Kennington, Oxford; Editor of 'The Annotated Book of Common Prayer,' etc.

Crown 8vo. 3s. 6d.

THE POPE AND THE COUNCIL.

By **Janus.** Authorized Translation from the German.

Third Edition, revised. Crown 8vo. 7s. 6d.

The CHURCH of GOD and the BISHOPS:

An Essay suggested by the Convocation of the Vatican Council. By **Henry St. A. Von Liaño.** Authorized Translation.

Crown 8vo. 4s. 6d.

LONDON, OXFORD, & CAMBRIDGE.

LETTERS FROM ROME on the COUNCIL.

By **Quirinus.** Reprinted from the *Allgemeine Zeitung.*
Authorized Translation.

The First Series contains Preliminary History of the Council and
Letters I. to XV.

The Second Series contains Letters XVI. to XXXIV.

Crown 8vo. 3s. 6d. each.

The Third Series, completing the Volume, is just ready.

THE AMMERGAU PASSION PLAY.

Reprinted by permission from the *Times.* With some Introductory
Remarks on the Origin and Development of Miracle Plays,
and some Practical Hints for the use of Intending Visitors.

By the Rev. **Malcolm MacColl,** M.A., Chaplain to the Right Hon.
Lord Napier, K.T.

Second Edition. Crown 8vo. 2s. 6d.

The FIRST BOOK OF COMMON PRAYER

OF EDWARD VI. AND THE ORDINAL OF 1549;

Together with the Order of the Communion, 1548.

Reprinted entire, and Edited by the Rev. **Henry Baskerville Walton,**
M.A., late Fellow and Tutor of Merton College.

With Introduction by the Rev. **Peter Goldsmith Medd,** M.A.,
Senior Fellow and Tutor of University College, Oxford.

Small 8vo. 6s.

THE PURSUIT OF HOLINESS.

A Sequel to 'Thoughts on Personal Religion,' intended to carry the
Reader somewhat farther onward in the Spiritual Life.

By **Edward Meyrick Goulburn,** D.D., Dean of Norwich.

Second Edition. Small 8vo. 5s.

LONDON, OXFORD, & CAMBRIDGE.

APOSTOLICAL SUCCESSION IN THE CHURCH OF ENGLAND.

By the Rev. **Arthur W. Haddan**, B.D., Rector of Barton-on-the-Heath, and late Fellow of Trinity College, Oxford.

8vo. 12s.

THE PRIEST TO THE ALTAR;

Or, Aids to the Devout Celebration of Holy Communion ; chiefly after the Ancient Use of Sarum.

Second Edition. Enlarged, Revised, and Re-arranged with the Secretæ, Post-communion, etc., appended to the Collects, Epistles, and Gospels, throughout the Year.

8vo. 7s. 6d.

NEWMAN'S (J. H.) PAROCHIAL AND PLAIN SERMONS.

Edited by the Rev. **W. J. Copeland**, Rector of Farnham, Essex.

From the Text of the last Editions published by Messrs. Rivington.

Eight vols. Crown 8vo. 5s. each.

NEWMAN'S (J. H.) SERMONS, BEARING UPON SUBJECTS OF THE DAY.

Edited by the Rev. **W. J. Copeland**, Rector of Farnham, Essex.

From the Text of the last Edition published by Messrs. Rivington. With Index of Dates of all the Sermons.

Printed uniformly with the 'Parochial and Plain Sermons.'

Crown 8vo. 5s.

BRIGHSTONE SERMONS.

By **George Moberly**, D.C.L., Bishop of Salisbury.

Second Edition. Crown 8vo. 7s. 6d.

LONDON, OXFORD, & CAMBRIDGE.

The CHARACTERS of the OLD TESTAMENT.

In a Series of Sermons.

By the Rev. **Isaac Williams**, B.D., late Fellow of Trinity College, Oxford.

New Edition. Crown 8vo. 5s.

FEMALE CHARACTERS of HOLY SCRIPTURE.

In a Series of Sermons.

By the Rev. **Isaac Williams**, B.D., late Fellow of Trinity College, Oxford.

New Edition. Crown 8vo. 5s.

THE DIVINITY OF OUR LORD AND SAVIOUR JESUS CHRIST:

Being the Bampton Lectures for 1866.

By **Henry Parry Liddon**, D.C.L., Canon of St. Paul's, and Ireland Professor of Exegesis in the University of Oxford.

Fourth Edition. Crown 8vo. 5s.

SERMONS PREACHED BEFORE THE UNIVERSITY OF OXFORD.

By **Henry Parry Liddon**, D.C.L., Canon of St. Paul's, and Ireland Professor of Exegesis in the University of Oxford.

Third Edition, revised. Crown 8vo. 5s.

A MANUAL FOR THE SICK;

With other Devotions.

By **Launcelot Andrewes**, D.D., sometime Lord Bishop of Winchester.

Edited, with a Preface, by **Henry Parry Liddon**, D.C.L., Canon of St. Paul's.

With Portrait. Second Edition. Large type. **24mo. 2s. 6d.**

LONDON, OXFORD, & CAMBRIDGE.

WALTER KERR HAMILTON: BISHOP of SALISBURY.

A Sketch, Reprinted, with Additions and Corrections, from the *Guardian*.

By **Henry Parry Liddon**, D.C.L., Canon of St. Paul's.

Second Edition. 8vo. *Limp cloth,* 2s. 6d.

Or, bound with the Sermon, 'Life in Death,' 3s. 6d.

THE LIFE OF MADAME LOUISE DE FRANCE,

Daughter of Louis XV., also known as the Mother Térèse de S. Augustin. By the Author of 'Tales of Kirkbeck.'

Crown 8vo. 6s.

JOHN WESLEY'S PLACE IN CHURCH HISTORY DETERMINED,

With the aid of Facts and Documents unknown to, or unnoticed by, his Biographers.

With a New and Authentic Portrait.

By **R. Denny Urlin**, M.R.I.A., of the Middle Temple, Barrister-at-Law.

Small 8vo. 5s. 6d.

THE TREASURY OF DEVOTION:

A Manual of Prayers for General and Daily Use.

Compiled by a Priest. Edited by the Rev. **T. T. Carter**, M.A., Rector of Clewer, Berks.

Third Edition. 16mo, *limp cloth* 2s.; *cloth extra*, 2s. 6d.

Bound with the Book of Common Prayer, 3s. 6d.

LONDON, OXFORD, & CAMBRIDGE.

THE GUIDE TO HEAVEN:

A Book of Prayers for every Want.   (For the Working Classes.)
Compiled by a Priest.   Edited by the Rev. **T. T. Carter**, M.A.,
Rector of Clewer, Berks.

Crown 8vo, limp cloth, 1s. ; *cloth extra,* 1s. 6d.

A DOMINICAN ARTIST:

A Sketch of the Life of the Rev. Père Besson, of the Order of
St. Dominic.
By the Author of 'Tales of Kirkbeck,' 'The Life of
Madame Louise de France,' etc.

Crown 8vo.   9s.

THE REFORMATION OF THE CHURCH
OF ENGLAND;

Its History, Principles, and Results.   A.D. 1514-1547.

By **John Henry Blunt**, M.A., Vicar of Kennington, Oxford, Editor
of 'The Annotated Book of Common Prayer,' Author of
'Directorium Pastorale,' etc., etc.

Second Edition.   8vo.   16s.

THE VIRGIN'S LAMP:

Prayers and Devout Exercises for English Sisters, chiefly composed
and selected by the late Rev. **J. M. Neale**, D.D., Founder of
St. Margaret's, East Grinsted.

Small 8vo.   3s. 6d.

CATECHETICAL NOTES AND CLASS
QUESTIONS, LITERAL & MYSTICAL;

Chiefly on the Earlier Books of Holy Scripture.

By the late Rev. **J. M. Neale**, D.D., Warden of Sackville College,
East Grinsted.

Crown 8vo.   5s.

LONDON, OXFORD, & CAMBRIDGE.

SERMONS FOR CHILDREN:

Being Thirty-three short Readings, addressed to the Children of
St. Margaret's Home, East Grinsted.

By the late Rev. **J. M. Neale**, D.D., Warden of Sackville College.

Second Edition. Small 8vo. 3s. 6d.

THE WITNESS of the OLD TESTAMENT TO CHRIST.

The Boyle Lectures for the Year 1868.

By the Rev. **Stanley Leathes**, M.A., Professor of Hebrew in King's
College, London, and Minister of St. Philip's, Regent Street.

8vo. 9s.

THE WITNESS of ST. PAUL to CHRIST:

Being the Boyle Lectures for 1869.

With an Appendix, on the Credibility of the Acts, in Reply to
the Recent Strictures of Dr. Davidson.

By the Rev. **Stanley Leathes**, M.A., Professor of Hebrew in King's
College, London, and Minister of St. Philip's, Regent Street.

8vo. 10s. 6d.

HONORÉ DE BALZAC.

Edited, with English Notes and Introductory Notice, by **Henri Van
Laun**, formerly French Master at Cheltenham College, and
now Master of the French Language and Literature at
the Edinburgh Academy.

(BEING THE FIRST VOLUME OF 'SELECTIONS FROM MODERN FRENCH AUTHORS.')

Crown 8vo. 3s. 6d.

LONDON, OXFORD, & CAMBRIDGE.

MESSRS. RIVINGTON'S NEW PUBLICATIONS.

H. A. TAINE.

Edited, with English Notes and Introductory Notice, by **Henri Van Laun,** formerly French Master at Cheltenham College, and now Master of the French Language and Literature at the Edinburgh Academy.

[BEING THE SECOND VOLUME OF 'SELECTIONS FROM MODERN FRENCH AUTHORS.']

Crown 8vo.   3s. 6d.

DEAN ALFORD'S GREEK TESTAMENT.

With English Notes, intended for the Upper Forms of Schools, and for Pass-men at the Universities.

Abridged by **Bradley H. Alford,** M.A., late Scholar of Trinity College, Cambridge.

Crown 8vo.   10s. 6d.

ELEMENTARY ALGEBRA.

By **J. Hamblin Smith,** M.A, Gonville and Caius College, and Lecturer at St. Peter's College, Cambridge.

New Edition, Revised and Enlarged.   Crown 8vo.   4s. 6d.

ELEMENTARY TRIGONOMETRY.

By **J. Hamblin Smith,** M.A., Gonville and Caius College, and Lecturer at St. Peter's College, Cambridge.

Third Edition, Revised and Enlarged.   Crown 8vo.   4s. 6d.

ELEMENTARY STATICS.

By **J. Hamblin Smith,** M.A., Gonville and Caius College, and Lecturer at St. Peter's College, Cambridge.

Royal 8vo.   5s.

LONDON, OXFORD, & CAMBRIDGE.

14

ELEMENTARY HYDROSTATICS.

By **J. Hamblin Smith**, M.A., Gonville and Caius College, and
Lecturer at St. Peter's College, Cambridge.

Second Edition, Revised and Enlarged. Crown 8vo. 3s.

EXERCISES ADAPTED TO ALGEBRA.

PART I.

By **J. Hamblin Smith**, M.A., Gonville and Caius College; and
Lecturer at St. Peter's College, Cambridge.

Crown 8vo. 2s. 6d.

ELEMENTS OF EUCLID,

Arranged with the Abbreviations admitted in the Cambridge
Examinations, and with Exercises.

By **J. Hamblin Smith**, M.A., Gonville and Caius College; and
Lecturer at St. Peter's College, Cambridge.

Crown 8vo. [*In the Press.*

ARITHMETIC, THEORETICAL AND PRACTICAL.

By **W. H. Girdlestone**, M.A., of Christ's College, Cambridge,
Principal of the Theological College, Gloucester.

New and Revised Edition. Crown 8vo. 6s. 6d.

Also an Edition for Schools. *Small 8vo. 3s. 6d.*

CLASSICAL EXAMINATION PAPERS.

Edited, with Notes and References, by **P. J. F. Gantillon**, M.A.,
sometime Scholar of St. John's College, Cambridge;
Classical Master in Cheltenham College.

Crown 8vo. 7s. 6d. Or interleaved with writing-paper for Notes,
half-bound, 10s. 6d.

LONDON, OXFORD, & CAMBRIDGE.

THE STORY OF THE GOSPELS.

In a single Narrative, combined from the Four Evangelists, showing in a new translation their unity. To which is added, a like continuous narrative in the Original Greek.

By the Rev. **William Pound**, M.A., late Fellow of St. John's College. Cambridge; Principal of Appulddurcombe School, Isle of Wight.

Two vols. 8vo. 36s.

THE LYRICS OF HORACE.

Done into English Rhyme.

By **Thomas Charles Baring**, M.A., late Fellow of Brasenose College, Oxford.

Small 4to. 7s.

A PLAIN AND SHORT HISTORY OF ENGLAND FOR CHILDREN.

In Letters from a Father to his Son. With a Set of Questions at the end of each Letter.

By **George Davys**, D.D., late Bishop of Peterborough.

New Edition, with Twelve Coloured Illustrations.
Square Crown 8vo. 3s. 6d.

A Cheap Edition for Schools, with portrait of Edward VI.
18mo. 1s. 6d.

HISTORY OF THE COLLEGE OF ST. JOHN THE EVANGELIST, CAMBRIDGE.

By **Thomas Baker**, B.D., Ejected Fellow.
Edited for the Syndics of the University Press, by **John E. B. Mayor**, M.A., Fellow of St. John's College.

Two vols. 8vo. 24s.

LONDON, OXFORD, & CAMBRIDGE.

MEMOIR OF THE RIGHT REV. JOHN
STRACHAN, D.D., LL.D., First Bishop of Toronto.
By **A. N. Bethune**, D.D., D.C.L., his Successor in the See.

8vo. 10s.

THE PRAYER BOOK INTERLEAVED;
With Historical Illustrations and Explanatory Notes arranged parallel to the Text.

By the Rev. **W. M. Campion**, D.D., Fellow and Tutor of Queen's College, and Rector of St. Botolph's, and the Rev. **W. J. Beamont**, M.A., late Fellow of Trinity College, Cambridge.

With a Preface by the **Lord Bishop of Ely.**

Fifth Edition. Small 8vo. 7s. 6d.

CONSOLING THOUGHTS IN SICKNESS.
Edited by **Henry Bailey**, B.D., Warden of St. Augustine's College, Canterbury.

Large type. Fine Edition. Small 8vo. 2s. 6d.

Also a Cheap Edition, 1s. 6d.; or in paper cover, 1s.

SICKNESS; ITS TRIALS & BLESSINGS.
New Edition, Small 8vo. 3s. 6d.

Also a Cheap Edition, 1s. 6d.; or in paper cover, 1s.

HYMNS AND POEMS FOR THE SICK
AND SUFFERING;
In connection with the Service for the Visitation of the Sick. Selected from various Authors.

Edited by **T. V. Fosbery**, M.A., Vicar of St. Giles's, Reading.

New Edition. Small 8vo. 3s. 6d.

HELP AND COMFORT FOR THE SICK
POOR.

By the Author of 'Sickness; its Trials and Blessings.'

New Edition. Small 8vo. 1s.

THE DOGMATIC FAITH:

An Inquiry into the relation subsisting between Revelation and Dogma. Being the Bampton Lectures for 1867.

By **Edward Garbett**, M.A., Incumbent of Christ Church, Surbiton.

Second Edition. Crown 8vo. 7s. 6d.

SKETCHES OF THE RITES & CUSTOMS
OF THE GRECO-RUSSIAN CHURCH.

By **H. C. Romanoff**. With an Introductory Notice by the Author of 'The Heir of Redclyffe.'

Second Edition. Crown 8vo. 7s. 6d.

HOUSEHOLD THEOLOGY:

A Handbook of Religious Information respecting the Holy Bible, the Prayer Book, the Church, the Ministry, Divine Worship, the Creeds, etc., etc.

By **John Henry Blunt**, M.A.

Third Edition. Small 8vo. 3s. 6d.

CURIOUS MYTHS OF THE MIDDLE
AGES.

By **S. Baring-Gould**, M.A., Author of 'Post-Mediæval Preachers,' etc. With Illustrations.

Complete in one Volume.

New Edition. Crown 8vo. 6s.

LONDON, OXFORD, & CAMBRIDGE.

13

SOI-MÊME; a Story of a Wilful Life.
Small 8vo.   3s. 6d.

THE HAPPINESS OF THE BLESSED,

Considered as to the Particulars of their State: their Recognition of each other in that State: and its Differences of Degrees.

To which are added, Musings on the Church and her Services.

By **Richard Mant**, D.D., sometime Lord Bishop of Down & Connor.

New Edition.   Small 8vo.   3s. 6d.

THE HOLY BIBLE.

With Notes and Introductions.

By **Chr. Wordsworth**, D.D., Bishop of Lincoln.

Imperial 8vo.

VOLUME I.   38s.

PART		£	s.	d.
I. Genesis and Exodus. *Second Edition* . . .		1	1	0
II. Leviticus, Numbers, Deuteronomy. *Second Edit.*		0	18	0

VOLUME II.   21s.

		£	s.	d.
III. Joshua, Judges, Ruth. *Second Edition* . .		0	12	0
IV. The Book of Samuel. *Second Edition* . .		0	10	0

VOLUME III.   21s.

		£	s.	d.
V. The Books of Kings, Chronicles, Ezra, Nehemiah, Esther. *Second Edition*		1	1	0

VOLUME IV.   34s.

		£	s.	d.
VI. The Book of Job. *Second Edition* . . .		0	9	0
VII. The Book of Psalms. *Second Edition* . . .		0	15	0
VIII. Proverbs, Ecclesiastes, Song of Solomon . .		0	12	0

VOLUME V.   32s. 6d.

		£	s.	d.
IX. Isaiah		0	12	6
X. Jeremiah, Lamentations, and Ezekiel . . .		1	1	0

VOLUME VI.

		£	s.	d.
XI. Daniel. (*In Preparation.*)				
XII. The Minor Prophets		0	12	0

LONDON, OXFORD, & CAMBRIDGE.

MISCELLANEOUS POEMS.

By Henry Francis Lyte, M.A.

New Edition.   Small 8vo.   5s.

PERRANZABULOE, THE LOST CHURCH FOUND;

Or, The Church of England not a New Church, but Ancient, Apostolical, and Independent, and a Protesting Church Nine Hundred Years before the Reformation.

By the Rev. **C. T. Collins Trelawny**, M.A., formerly Rector of Timsbury, Somerset, and late Fellow of Balliol College, Oxford.

With Illustrations.   New Edition.   Crown 8vo.   3s. 6d.

CATECHESIS; or, CHRISTIAN INSTRUCTION

Preparatory to Confirmation and First Communion.

By **Charles Wordsworth**, D.C.L., Bishop of St. Andrew's.

New Edition.   Small 8vo.   2s.

WARNINGS OF THE HOLY WEEK, etc.;

Being a Course of Parochial Lectures for the Week before Easter and the Easter Festivals.

By the Rev. **W. Adams**, M.A., late Vicar of St. Peter's-in-the-East, Oxford, and Fellow of Merton College.

Sixth Edition.   Small 8vo.   4s. 6d.

CONSOLATIO; OR, COMFORT FOR THE AFFLICTED.

Edited by the Rev. **C. E. Kennaway**. With a Preface by **Samuel Wilberforce**, D.D., Lord Bishop of Winchester.

New Edition.   Small 8vo.   3s. 6d.

THE HILLFORD CONFIRMATION: a Tale.
By M. C. Phillpotts.
18mo. 1*s.*

FROM MORNING TO EVENING:
A Book for Invalids.
From the French of M. L'Abbé Henri Perreyve.
Translated and adapted by an Associate of the Sisterhood of
S. John Baptist, Clewer.
Crown 8vo. 5*s.*

FAMILY PRAYERS;
Compiled from Various Sources (chiefly from Bishop Hamilton's
Manual), and arranged on the Liturgical Principle.
By Edward Meyrick Goulburn, D.D., Dean of Norwich.
New Edition. Crown 8vo, large type, 3*s.* 6*d.*
Cheap Edition. 16*mo.* 1*s.*

THE ANNUAL REGISTER:
A Review of Public Events at Home and Abroad, for the Year 1869;
being the Seventh Volume of an Improved Series.
8vo. 18*s.*

⁎⁎⁎ The Volumes for 1863 *to* 1868 *may be had, price* 18*s. each.*

A PROSE TRANSLATION OF VIRGIL'S
ECLOGUES AND GEORGICS.
By an Oxford Graduate.
Crown 8vo. 2*s.* 6*d.*

THE CAMBRIDGE PARAGRAPH BIBLE
OF THE AUTHORIZED ENGLISH VERSION.

With the Text Revised by a Collation of its Early and other
Principal Editions, the Use of the Italic type made Uniform,
the Marginal References Re-modelled, and a Critical
Introduction prefixed.

By the Rev. **F. H. Scrivener**, M.A., Rector of St. Gerrans; Editor
of the Greek Testament, Codex Augiensis, etc.   Edited
for the Syndics of the University Press.

Crown 4to.

Part I., Genesis to Solomon's Song, 15s.

Part II., Apocrypha and New Testament, 15s.

To be completed in Three Parts.

Part III., Prophetical Books, will be ready about May, 1871.

** A small number of copies has also been printed, on *good
writing paper*, with one column of print and wide margin to
each page for MS. notes. *Part I.*, 20s.; *Part II.*, 20s.

QUIET MOMENTS:

A Four Weeks' Course of Thoughts and Meditations,
before Evening Prayer and at Sunset.

By Lady Charlotte Maria Pepys.

New Edition.   Small 8vo.   2s. 6d.

MORNING NOTES OF PRAISE:
A Series of Meditations upon the Morning Psalms.

By Lady Charlotte Maria Pepys.

New Edition.   Small 8vo.   2s. 6d.

LONDON, OXFORD, & CAMBRIDGE.

22

YESTERDAY, TO-DAY, AND FOR EVER;

A Poem in Twelve Books.

By **Edward Henry Bickersteth**, M.A., vicar of Christ Church, Hampstead, and Chaplain to the Bishop of Ripon.

Fourth Edition. Small 8vo. 6s.

THE COMMENTARIES OF GAIUS:

Translated, with Notes, by **J. T. Abdy**, LL.D., Regius Professor of Laws in the University of Cambridge, and Barrister-at-Law of the Norfolk Circuit: formerly Fellow of Trinity Hall; and **Bryan Walker**, M.A., M.L.; Fellow and Lecturer of Corpus Christi College, and Law Lecturer of St. John's College, Cambridge; formerly Law Student of Trinity Hall and Chancellor's Legal Medallist.

Crown 8vo. 12s. 6d.

SACRED ALLEGORIES:

The Shadow of the Cross—The Distant Hills—The Old Man's Home—The King's Messengers.

By the Rev. **W. Adams**, M.A., late Fellow of Merton College, Oxford.

Presentation Edition. With Engravings from original designs by Charles W. Cope, R.A., John C. Horsley, A.R.A., Samuel Palmer, Birket Foster, and George Hicks.

Small 4to. 10s. 6d.

The Four Allegories, separately. *Crown 8vo. 2s. 6d. each.*

HERBERT TRESHAM:

A Tale of the Great Rebellion.

By the late Rev. **J. M. Neale**, D.D., sometime Scholar of Trinity College, Cambridge, and late Warden of Sackville College, East Grinsted.

New Edition. Small 8vo. 3s. 6d.

THE MANOR FARM: a Tale.

By **M. C. Phillpotts**, Author of 'The Hillford Confirmation.'

With Four Illustrations. Small 8vo. 3s. 6d.

LONDON, OXFORD, & CAMBRIDGE.

LIBER PRECUM PUBLICARUM
ECCLESIÆ ANGLICANÆ.

A Gulielmo Bright, A.M., et Petro Goldsmith Medd, A.M.,
Presbyteris, Collegii Universitatis in Acad. Oxon.
Sociis, Latine redditus.

New Edition, with all the Rubrics in red. Small 8vo. 6s.

BIBLE READINGS FOR FAMILY PRAYER.

By the Rev. **W. H. Ridley**, M.A., Rector of Hambleden.

Crown 8vo.

Old Testament—Genesis and Exodus.   2s.

New Testament, 3s. 6d. { St. Matthew and St. Mark.   2s.
{ St. Luke and St. John.   2s.

INSTRUCTIONS FOR THE USE OF
CANDIDATES FOR HOLY ORDERS,

And of the Parochial Clergy; with Acts of Parliament relating to
the same, and Forms proposed to be used.

By **Christopher Hodgson**, M.A., Secretary to the Governors of
Queen Anne's Bounty.

Ninth Edition, Revised and Enlarged, 8vo.   16s.

ENGLAND RENDERED IMPREGNABLE

By the practical Military Organization and efficient Equipment of her
National Forces; and her Present Position, Armament, Coast
Defences, Administration, and Future Power considered.

By **H. A. L.**, 'The Old Shekarry.'

8vo.   *[Nearly ready.*

CATENA CLASSICORUM:

A SERIES OF CLASSICAL AUTHORS,

EDITED BY MEMBERS OF BOTH UNIVERSITIES UNDER THE DIRECTION OF

THE REV. ARTHUR HOLMES, M.A.,

Fellow and Lecturer of Clare College, Cambridge, Lecturer and Late Fellow of St. John's College;

AND

THE REV. CHARLES BIGG, M.A.,

Late Senior Student and Tutor of Christ Church, Oxford, Second Classical Master of Cheltenham College.

Crown 8vo.

THE FOLLOWING PARTS HAVE BEEN ALREADY PUBLISHED :—

SOPHOCLIS TRAGOEDIAE.

Edited by R. C. JEBB, M.A., Fellow and Assistant Tutor of Trinity College, Cambridge, and Public Orator of the University,
The Electra, 3s. 6d.   The Ajax, 3s. 6d.

JUVENALIS SATIRAE.

Edited by G. A. SIMCOX, M.A., Fellow and Classical Lecturer of Queen's College, Oxford.
3s. 6d.

THUCYDIDIS HISTORIA.

Edited by CHARLES BIGG, M.A, late Senior Student and Tutor of Christ Church, Oxford.   Second Classical Master of Cheltenham College.
Books I. and II. with Introductions.   6s.

LONDON, OXFORD, & CAMBRIDGE.

DEMOSTHENIS ORATIONES PUBLICAE.

Edited by G. H. HESLOP, M.A., Late Fellow and Assistant Tutor of Queen's College, Oxford.   Head Master of St. Bees.

The Olynthiacs and the Philippics.   4s. 6d.

ARISTOPHANIS COMOEDIAE.

Edited by W. C. GREEN, M.A., late Fellow of King's College, Cambridge.   Classical Lecturer at Queen's College.

The Acharnians and the Knights.   4s.
The Clouds.   3s. 6d.
The Wasps.   3s. 6d.

An Edition of the Archarnians and the Knights, Revised and especially adapted for Use in Schools.   4s.

ISOCRATIS ORATIONES.

Edited by JOHN EDWIN SANDYS, M.A., Fellow and Tutor of St. John's College, and Classical Lecturer at Jesus College, Cambridge.

Ad Demonicum et Panegyricus.   4s. 6d.

PERSII SATIRAE.

Edited by A. PRETOR, M.A., of Trinity College, Cambridge, Classical Lecturer of Trinity Hall.   3s. 6d.

HOMERI ILIAS.

Edited by S. H. REYNOLDS, M.A., Fellow and Tutor of Brasenose College, Oxford.

Books I. to XII.   6s.

TERENTI COMOEDIAE.

Edited by T. L. PAPILLON, M.A., Fellow and Classical Lecturer of Merton College, Oxford.

Andria et Eunuchus.   4s. 6d.

LONDON, OXFORD, & CAMBRIDGE.

KEYS TO CHRISTIAN KNOWLEDGE.

Small 8vo.   2s. 6d. each.

A KEY TO THE KNOWLEDGE AND USE OF THE BOOK OF COMMON PRAYER.

By **John Henry Blunt**, M.A.

A KEY TO THE KNOWLEDGE AND USE OF THE HOLY BIBLE.

By **John Henry Blunt**, M.A.

A KEY TO THE KNOWLEDGE OF CHURCH HISTORY (ANCIENT).

Edited by **John Henry Blunt**, M.A.

A KEY TO THE NARRATIVE OF THE FOUR GOSPELS.

By **John Pilkington Norris**, M.A., Canon of Bristol, formerly one of Her Majesty's Inspectors of Schools.

A KEY TO THE KNOWLEDGE OF CHURCH HISTORY (MODERN).

Edited by **John Henry Blunt**, M.A.

A KEY TO CHRISTIAN DOCTRINE & PRACTICE.

(Founded on the Church Catechism.)

By **John Henry Blunt**, M.A.

LONDON, OXFORD, & CAMBRIDGE.

RIVINGTON'S DEVOTIONAL SERIES.

Elegantly printed with red borders. 16mo. 2s. 6d.

THOMAS À KEMPIS, OF THE IMITATION OF CHRIST.

Also a cheap Edition, without the red borders, 1s., or in Cover, 6d.

THE RULE AND EXERCISES OF HOLY LIVING.

By **Jeremy Taylor**, D.D., Bishop of Down, and Connor, and Dromore.

Also a cheap Edition, without the red borders, 1s.

THE RULE AND EXERCISES OF HOLY DYING.

By **Jeremy Taylor**, D.D., Bishop of Down, and Connor, and Dromore,

Also a cheap Edition, without the red borders, 1s.

*** The 'Holy Living' and the 'Holy Dying' may be had bound together in One Volume, 5s., or without the red borders, 2s. 6d.

A SHORT AND PLAIN INSTRUCTION

For the better Understanding of the Lord's Supper; to which is annexed, the Office of the Holy Communion, with proper Helps and Directions.

By **Thomas Wilson**, D.D., late Lord Bishop of Sodor and Man.

Complete Edition, in large type.

Also a cheap Edition, without the red borders, 1s., or in Cover, 6d.

INTRODUCTION TO THE DEVOUT LIFE.

From the French of St. Francis of Sales, Bishop and Prince of Geneva. A New Translation.

A PRACTICAL TREATISE CONCERNING EVIL THOUGHTS.

By **William Chilcot**, M.A.

ENGLISH POEMS AND PROVERBS.

By **George Herbert.**

LONDON, OXFORD, & CAMBRIDGE.

THE 'ASCETIC LIBRARY:'

A Series of Translations of Spiritual Works for Devotional
Reading from Catholic Sources.

Edited by the Rev. **Orby Shipley,** M.A.

Square Crown 8vo.

THE MYSTERIES OF MOUNT CALVARY.

Translated from the Latin of **Antonio de Guevara.** 3*s.* 6*d.*

PREPARATION FOR DEATH.

Translated from the Italian of **Alfonso,** Bishop of S. Agatha. 5*s.*

COUNSELS ON HOLINESS OF LIFE.

Translated from the Spanish of ' The Sinner's Guide ' by
Luis de Granada. 5*s.*

EXAMINATION OF CONSCIENCE UPON SPECIAL SUBJECTS.

Translated and Abridged from the French of **Tronson.** 5*s.*

LONDON, OXFORD, & CAMBRIDGE.

NEW PAMPHLETS.

BY ARCHDEACON BICKERSTETH.

A CHARGE,

Delivered at his Eleventh Visitation of the Archdeaconry of
Buckingham, in May and June, 1870.

8vo. 1*s.*

THE RESURRECTION OF THE BODY:

A Sermon, preached in the Parish Church of Horsendon, on the
Second Sunday after Easter, 1870, on the occasion of the
Death of Lucy Olivia Hobart, wife of the Rev.
W. E. Partridge, of Horsendon House, Bucks.

8vo. 1*s.*

BY THE REV. F. GARDEN.

CAN AN ORDAINED MAN BECOME A LAYMAN?

Some Remarks on Mr. Herbert's Bill.

8vo. 6*d.*

THE ARNOLD HISTORICAL ESSAY, 1870.

THE SCYTHIC NATIONS,

Down to the Fall of the Western Empire.

By JOHN GENT, B.A., Fellow of Trinity College, Oxford.

8vo. 2*s.*

BY THE REV. A. PERCEVAL PUREY CUST.

OUR COMMON FRAILTY:

A Sermon, preached in the Parish Church of St. Lawrence, Reading,
on Quinquagesima Sunday, February 27, 1870, at the
Opening of the Spring Assize.

8vo. 6*d.*

BY THE REV. W. B. GALLOWAY.

'OUR HOLY AND OUR BEAUTIFUL HOUSE.'

A Sermon preached at Dunstable, on Sunday, May 22, 1870, on
behalf of the Restoration of Dunstable Church.

8vo. 6*d.*

LONDON, OXFORD, & CAMBRIDGE.

New Pamphlets—*continued.*

BY THE RIGHT HON. SIR ROBERT PHILLIMORE, D.C.L.

JUDGMENT,

Delivered by The Right Hon. Sir Robert Phillimore, D.C.L., Official Principal of the Arches Court of Canterbury, in the case of the Office of the Judge promoted by Sheppard *v.* Bennett.

Edited by WALTER G. F. PHILLIMORE, B.C.L., of the Middle Temple, Barrister-at-Law; Fellow of All Souls' College, and Vinerian Scholar, Oxford.

8vo. 2s. 6d.

BY CANON LIDDON.

PAUPERISM AND THE LOVE OF GOD:

A Sermon, preached at St. Paul's, Knightsbridge, on the Second Sunday after Trinity, 1870, for the Convalescent Hospital at Ascot.

8vo. 1s.

HOW TO DO GOOD:

A Sermon, preached in the Cathedral Church of St. Paul, May 18, 1870, at the Two Hundred and Sixteenth Anniversary Festival of the Sons of the Clergy.

8vo. 6d.

THE MODEL OF OUR NEW LIFE.

A Sermon, preached at the Special Evening Service in St. Paul's Cathedral on Easter Day, 1870.

8vo. 3d., or 2s. 6d. per dozen.

BY THE REV. E. H. BICKERSTETH.

JESUS AND THE RESURRECTION;

Or, the Ministry of the Church a Witness for the Resurrection. A Paper read before the Diocesan Conference of Clergy in the Convocation House, Oxford, July, 1869.

8vo. 6d.

BY CANON BRIGHT.

CHRIST'S PRESENCE AMID THEOLOGICAL STUDIES.

A Sermon, preached in the Parish Church of Cuddesdon, on the Anniversary Festival of Cuddesdon College, June 14, 1870.

8vo. 6d.

LONDON, OXFORD, & CAMBRIDGE.

31

Eight Volumes, Crown 8vo, 5s. each.

A New and Uniform Edition of
A DEVOTIONAL COMMENTARY
ON THE
GOSPEL NARRATIVE.

BY THE
REV. ISAAC WILLIAMS, B.D.
FORMERLY FELLOW OF TRINITY COLLEGE, OXFORD.

—oo—

THOUGHTS ON THE STUDY OF THE HOLY GOSPELS.
Characteristic Differences in the Four Gospels—Our Lord's Manifestations of Himself—The Rule of Scriptural Interpretation Furnished by Our Lord —Analogies of the Gospel —Mention of Angels in the Gospels—Places of Our Lord's Abode and Ministry—Our Lord's Mode of Dealing with His Apostles—Conclusion.

A HARMONY OF THE FOUR EVANGELISTS.
Our Lord's Nativity—Our Lord's Ministry (Second Year)—Our Lord's Ministry (Third Year)—The Holy Week—Our Lord's Passion—Our Lord's Resurrection.

OUR LORD'S NATIVITY.
The Birth at Bethlehem—The Baptism in Jordan—The First Passover.

OUR LORD'S MINISTRY. SECOND YEAR.
The Second Passover—Christ with the Twelve—The Twelve sent Forth.

OUR LORD'S MINISTRY. THIRD YEAR.
Teaching in Galilee—Teaching at Jerusalem—Last Journey from Galilee to Jerusalem.

THE HOLY WEEK.
The Approach to Jerusalem—The Teaching in the Temple—The Discourse on the Mount of Olives—The Last Supper.

OUR LORD'S PASSION.
The Hour of Darkness—The Agony—The Apprehension—The Condemnation—The Day of Sorrows—The Hall of Judgment—The Crucifixion—The Sepulture.

OUR LORD'S RESURRECTION.
The Day of Days—The Grave Visited—Christ Appearing—The Going to Emmaus — The Forty Days—The Apostles Assembled — The Lake in Galilee—The Mountain in Galilee—The Return from Galilee.

LONDON, OXFORD, & CAMBRIDGE.

www.ingramcontent.com/pod-product-compliance
Lightning Source LLC
Chambersburg PA
CBHW021754110726
47902CB00006B/1521